# Insanely In Love

**A novel**

**By**

**Cereka Cook**

**RJ Publications, LLC**

**Newark, New Jersey**

The characters and events in this book are fictitious. Any resemblance to actual persons, living or dead, is purely coincidental.

RJ Publications
**cmonet_@hotmail.com**
www.rjpublications.com

ISBN 978-0981777320



Printed in Canada

May 2009

1-2-3-4-5-6-7-8-9-10-11

# "Insanely In Love"

## BY

## Cereka Cook

# Acknowledgement

Jesse C. Martin Jr., Linda McCleskey, Tynisia Hanson, Steven T. Hanson, Tashekia Boone, Felecia Boone, Lisa Boone, Robert Boone, Lil' Robert, Sibba Boone, Harold and Leatha Boone, Ladaria Smith, Richard Jeanty, Marcus of Nubian Bookstore, G.A.A.L. book club, Martina Borden, Shonta Bass, Rawsistaz, Tee C. Royale, O.O.S.A. book club, Ms. Toni, LaShawna Morton, Oyin Jones-Mitchell, Sakonja Ragland, Quintricia Carpenter, all the former Delta Air Lines skycaps in Atlanta, Brian Overs, Lonnie Sanders, Lionel and Sherice Hemmons, Barron and Teri Walker, Sonya Lloyd, Stacey Campbell-Knighten, Craig Knighten, Kesha and Vince Haynie, AJ Manning, Earl Cook, Brenda Cook, Joanne Cook, Cash, Jeffery and Marline Cook, Stacy Cook and all the rest of the Cook fam (it's too many of us to mention) ;-)....Miriam Barnett, Mischelda Sapp, Torrian Ferguson, Jessica Milligan, Alicia Miller, Kim and El Beasley.

This is for all of you who have been instrumental in helping me progress to the next level. And for anyone that has given me kind words and poured positivity in my direction. For those of you whose name was not mentioned, let's use the old cliche, charge it to my head and not my heart. Thank you all from the bottom to the top of my heart. Smooches! (LaShawna thanks for letting me steal that!)

Love ya

CMC

## Chapter 1
## Rain Hunter

Men are a straight up trip. Contrary to what they believe, every woman does not want to be married and have children. I'm the perfect example. I enjoy my life. I'm twenty-nine years old, co-own Lena's Place (a restaurant) with my sister, drive a nice whip, live in an elite neighborhood located in the upper echelon of Atlanta, and I have a closet full of clothes that make me look like I could create my own version of *GQ Women magazine*. Now, why would I want to mess all that up?

Although, I can certainly understand why *any* man would want to get with me. Hell, I'm what they call a "triple-threat". I'm pretty, smart, and I have a body so tight, that I would put that video model, Melyssa Ford to shame. No plastic, no pills, no implants…just real.

Oh, by the way, I'm Rain, Rain Hunter. And I know what you're thinking. You're thinking that I'm arrogant and materialistic. Well, let me assure you, I'm not. I don't come off like that to most people. I just think a certain way in the privacy of my own mind. And as far as having nice things… there is nothing wrong with that.

I'm used to it. I became used to it as a child and now as an adult. I work for what I want and I refuse to apologize for having and enjoying nice shit. Please! Life is too short for all that.

As far as men are concerned, they like me and I like them. But I like a certain type of man. I like a suit and tie man, someone who mirrors me. My ideal man would probably drive a Mercedes or a Jaguar. That would mean he definitely has his own money, and that way he won't be all up in my pocket. He would definitely have his own home and would not have any children. I just don't have time to be playing mama. Besides that, I don't have time or even want to deal with no baby-mama-freakin'- drama. My sister says I need to get a real man. She says I need some thug passion in my life. She says, "What's the use of having a man if he can't fix shit around the house." I say, "Hell, if he has the money, he can call somebody to come and fix it."

But all joking aside, at this point in my life, I'm not looking to be committed to anyone. I just want to meet people, date and have fun. I do want to be married one day, just not now. He would definitely have to be very special and someone that would significantly change my life. What I didn't know, is that, I would soon meet someone that would change my life foreve

# Chapter 2
# Jack Anderson

*"Ooh my first mistake was, I wanted too much time...I had to have him morning, noon, and night."* I was listening to En Vogue playing on my favorite old-school station as I drove in to work. I love old school R&B and hip-hop. I was making hand and face gestures singing to myself in the mirror. I guess sitting at a red light, I had become oblivious to the cars behind me and the car next to me. I was into my own little world so much that I didn't notice the fine man to my left in the BMW. He liked what he saw and smiled at me until I finally looked around and took notice of who was watching. When our eyes locked, I immediately stopped dancing and singing. How embarrassing.

Saved by the green light, I made a left turn, as did my admirer. I sped away to the nearest gas station. As I got out of the car I noticed the same gentleman had pulled up to the pump in front of me. I tried to ignore him by not giving any eye contact. I could see everything he was doing in my peripheral vision. And from the looks of it, he was walking over in my direction. *Oh, oh don't look, don't look*, I thought.

As he walked toward me, I could feel him sizing me up. I could tell he thought I was fine. He summed me up in thirty seconds. *Hmm...S-Class Mercedes...she's got class and money, so she's independent. And she's got a body that she loves showing off, so she's confident, yet there's a certain modest air about her. And she's beautiful with beautiful black hair that only enhances that butterscotch complexion.*

Like most men, he was a sucker for a big butt and a smile.

"Excuse me," he said in a coy manner.

You know I had to play it off like I didn't see him approaching me.

"Yes?"

He started making the usual small talk that you make when you first meet someone. His name was Jack Anderson. I read it off the business card that he handed me. He was a stockbroker for a prestigious firm. Then it was my turn to size him up. I gotta give it to him. He was fine. He kinda reminded me of Boris Kodjoe. And he was wearing the hell out of that three-piece suit. It was a gray suit with a pink shirt. Real men can confidently wear pink – not that hot, flaming pink, but that nice pale pink.

"So, what's *your* name?" he finally asked me.

"Rain."
"Rain…hmm an interesting name." "That's a pretty name, but then you're a pretty woman." He began to pour on the charm like syrup on pancakes.
"Thanks." And all I could do was smile. He was smooth, but I'm not that easy. You have to work to get to know me.

He could tell that he really wasn't going to get anywhere with me, at least not today. He made up something about having to meet with a client. Then he made a statement in the form of a question about getting together for a drink.
"Sure," I told him. As soon as he drove off, I tossed his business card in the trash. He looked good, but I like dark skin brothas.

Once I was finished pumping gas, I sped down the freeway toward downtown. My cell phone was ringing. It was my favorite person in the whole world, my sister, Aaries. She and I did just about everything together. Actually, we acted more like best friends than sisters. Did I mention Aaries is also my identical twin? We get mistaken a lot, despite the fact that my hair is black and hers is dyed auburn. We're used to it, though. It goes with the territory. Anyway, we're only identical in DNA form. Our personalities are totally different. Believe it or not, I'm the more conservative one. She's a little more outgoing and a lot more dominant. That probably has something to do with the fact that she's older than me by nine minutes. People often ask us if we have this weird twin thing going on where we can feel each other's pain. We don't. But we are somewhat clairvoyant. For instance, if something is wrong with one of us the other one can sense it somehow. It's hard to explain, but I remember one time when we were in third grade, we were playing at school. It was during recess. I had to run to the bathroom and before I got out of the bathroom this funny feeling came over me like something had happened to Aaries. I ran back outside to see what had happened and she had fallen off of a swing and broken her arm. She was in a cast for a couple of months.

Aaries was calling to tell me that she wouldn't be able to make it in to work today.

"Why, what's wrong?"

"I don't know. My stomach hurts...probably something I ate. I'm sure I'll be fine."

"Okay, well get some rest and I'll take care of the books for you at the restaurant."

"No you won't," uttered Aaries.

Now why did I have to go and say that? Aaries almost had a fit. She told me to leave the bookkeeping to her. I am not good with numbers at all. The last time I tried to take care of the books, it took her a week to clean up one day of my mess.

"Just leave all the receipts on my desk and I'll take care of it tomorrow." "Alright, alright," I chuckled.

"Just stick to what you do best Rain…meeting and greeting the customers. You're the personable twin, and I'm the one everybody thinks is temperamental."

"You *are* temperamental," I told her matter of factly. "Whatever. I just keep it real. And I'm straight to the point." Rather than argue with my sister, I ended the conversation.

# Chapter 3
# Twins

I had just finished putting on my eye shadow when I heard a knock at the door. I wasn't expecting anyone. As I was approaching the door to see who it was, my lock was being pried open. Then the door began to open. I figured it was Aaries, since she was the only one, who had a key to my place, but I wanted to make sure and I wasn't taking any chances. I grabbed my Louisville Slugger that I kept underneath the couch.

"Hey sis, what's up? " Aaries inquired nonchalantly. I breathed a sigh of relief.

"Nothing, except that I see I need to get my locks changed. You scared me to death."

"Well who else would it be? I'm the only one with a spare key to your house."

"True. So what's up? What do you need?"

"What? Who said I needed anything? I might just want to visit."

"Whatever, Aaries...we're twins remember? I know you, probably better than you know yourself. Besides, why would you be visiting me when we see each other practically everyday at the restaurant? Now what gives?"

Aaries smiled because she knew I was right. "Well, you're right. I need to borrow your fondue set."
"Go ahead, you know where everything is. I need to finish getting ready," I said as I walked back into my bedroom.
Aaries took notice of my appearance and followed me into the bedroom. "And where are you going, looking like that Miss Thang? Look at you, cleavage showing....you got your back all out."
"Nowhere special. I'm just going up to *Twist* to meet Maliq."
"Maliq? Since when do you get all dolled up to see Maliq? Anything, you want to tell me?" she asked, with a wide grin on her face.
"You're trippin'. You know I like to look good wherever I go. Besides we're just going to meet for a few drinks that's all."
"Un-huh," Aaries stated suspiciously. "So when did you two start going on dates?"
"It's not a date, we're just meeting for a few drinks and conversation."
"Hmm....well last time I checked, that was called a date."
"Shut up," I told her as I pursed my lips together with my favorite lip-gloss. But I knew she was only kidding.
"It's cool with me, though. You know I've always liked Maliq with his LL Cool J lookin' fine

ass! You need to go on and hook up with him and make him part of the family." We laughed simultaneously.

"He's already a part of the family. And has been since we all went to junior high school together."

"You know what I mean. I mean make him part of the family officially."

"Oh, now I know you're trippin' Aaries. You know Maliq and I have been best friends since junior high. Besides...I don't even look at him that way."

"Yeah well, he looks at *you* that way. And who do you think you're fooling? Just like you told me earlier, we're twins remember? I know you just as well as I know myself. Maybe a little better. Are you trying to tell me that you're not attracted to Maliq at all? He's damn near the spitting image of LL. Body and all. And he's so sweet. Now tell me he's not a catch?"

"I didn't say he wasn't a catch." I continued to primp in the mirror and played with my hair. "I'm just saying we're friends and nothing more. Nor will we ever be more."

"Well, I have news for you little sister. Men and women cannot truly be *just friends.*"

I love my sister dearly, but she was starting to get on my nerves a little. "Didn't you come over here for that fondue set?"

"You're kicking me out huh? Ok, fine I'm leaving, but not before you let me fix your hair."
I did a double take in the mirror and frowned. "What's wrong with my hair?"
"Nothing, but you always wear that damn two-strand twist. Do something different like put some color in it like mine. Or at least wear it down for a change. Wear it wild."
"Nah, I like it like this."
"Alright, well you look beautiful anyway. And have a good time with Maliq," Aaries said sarcastically.
"Whatever Aaries," I told her as I looked at her through the bathroom mirror. "Anyway, what are you going to do with that fondue set?"
Aaries smiled somewhat blushingly. She and Dominic were celebrating their first anniversary on September 30th. She was trying to set the tone and make everything romantic. She wanted to hook up the fondue burner and set fresh fruit around it. They were going to have strawberries, pineapples, and peaches - the works.

Aaries was in love with her husband Dominic. Although they had only been married for a year, they had been exclusive four years prior. And Dominic was good for my sister. It seemed as if they had the perfect marriage, the perfect relationship. He doted on her and gave her whatever she wanted, and treated her like a queen.

Aaries definitely returned the favors and enjoyed every minute of it. She handled her business when it came down to her man.

Originally, they were supposed to cruise to the Caribbean for their anniversary. Aaries was worried about me having help at the restaurant. She said no one could run our family's business like we could. She had a point, but I told her not to worry about it, and that I could manage for a few days alone.

Shortly, after some idle chit-chat, she told me I was holding her up and that she needed to go, so she could handle her business.

Aaries winked and walked to the kitchen to get the fondue set. In a blink, she was gone.

# Chapter 4
# Best Friend

When I arrived at *Twist,* it seemed as though it took me fifteen minutes just to walk from the parking lot to the restaurant. Two different men, whom I turned down diplomatically, had approached me.

As I walked into the restaurant, I skimmed the place to look for Maliq. I couldn't find him so I pulled my cell phone out, searched for Maliq Carson, and mashed 'M' on my cell phone. Maliq said he was in the back of the restaurant in a booth.

As I approached the booth, Maliq noticed me and stood up to greet me with a hug. We both smiled when we saw each other.

"You look beautiful Rain."

"Thanks, you look good too."

Maliq tried very hard not to stare at my breasts. But it was too late I caught him. I guess that was just a man's nature. Whether I was his home girl or his wife, he was going to look. He couldn't help it. He had begun to notice when we went out the last few times, I was a little sexier than usual.

Maliq wore some comfortable fitting khaki pants with a black polo style shirt that revealed his muscular frame.

As soon as the server arrived, we ordered right away. I ordered some sushi with a top shelf gin and orange juice. At a restaurant or a bar, I made sure I said the brand I wanted; otherwise, they just gave you plain old gin and juice. And I wasn't in the mood for a headache. That's what the cheap stuff does to you. It makes your head ache. Maliq wanted a Heineken and some wings.

As the server was walking away, Maliq's cell phone rang. He looked at the caller id on the phone and shook his head.

I was pretty sure I knew who it was. There was only one person that got under his skin like that – his ex-wife Tasha. Maliq had gotten caught up and married to her. They were married for one year and have been divorced for two. During which time, they conceived a beautiful son named Jaden. Anytime she called, it was never for anything positive, and that's a shame considering that they share a child. I hated to see my friend being taken through so much drama. But I had his back no matter what.

"Look Tasha, you've pulled this shit too many times. Have my son ready tomorrow by ten o'clock or we're going to be in court very soon. Listen to you, cursing and yelling. Is that what

you've been teaching my son? I know he's yours too, but you need to start acting like a mother. What? Whatever Tasha....'bye!"
Maliq became frustrated with the phone call and hung up on her.
By this time, the server had come back with our drinks. She told us our appetizers would be ready shortly. We thanked her, and then she walked off.
"You okay?" I asked Maliq placing my hand on top of his.
"Not really, that's what I wanted to talk to you about."
I waited for Maliq to open up about his situation. He didn't trust many people, but he trusted me. After all, we've known each other since junior high school.
"Basically I'm tired of Tasha using Jaden and I. So I'm taking her to court. I want joint custody. He really just needs to be with me, but I know he needs his mother, too. I don't want to be selfish the way she has been, and tomorrow is the last straw. If I don't get to see Jaden...it's on! I'm going to fill the paper work out for family court." He took a large swig of his beer straight to the head.
I took my cue from Maliq and sipped on my gin and juice.
"So you don't think that if you talk with her she'll budge?"

"Please. She hasn't yet. And besides that, Tasha doesn't want me to have a life outside of her. Every time I try to get involved with someone, oh all of a sudden Jaden is sick, or she forgets she has something else planned for him. And then she says that she doesn't want any other women around him."

Although I couldn't relate to his situation, I sympathized with him and was a very supportive friend.

"Don't worry Maliq. You're a good man and an even better father. You know I got your back. If you need me as a character witness, just let me know."

Maliq cracked a faint smile.

"Thanks, that's why we've been friends so long. 'Cause you've always been supportive of me."

Several hours later we were both buzzed off of the liquor. As Maliq walked me to my car, he stared at my ass and quickly dismissed his thoughts as quickly as they had come. *It must be the liquor talking,* he thought.

"You gonna be alright to drive Maliq?"

"Yeah, I'm good. I'll be alright."

"Okay, well call me if you need me". I reached up to give him a hug; and although I stood 5'9'' in heels, Maliq was much taller. I still had to reach up to kiss his cheek. As I pulled away from him, his lips brushed mine just a little and my heart

starting beating fast, and I became a little moist. Our eyes locked briefly, and then we shook it off as though we were both in a trance. What in the world is going on? Why am I feeling like this with my best friend? With that I went on home.
"Call me when you make it in Rain."

## Chapter 5
## Imagine That

When Maliq got home, he immediately went upstairs and flopped down on his bed. He was emotionally drained. Just for tonight, he didn't want to think about his problems. He did, however, think about me in those tight jeans and that revealing halter top. *Damn*, he thought. His hand brushed his balls and then his manhood started to push his khaki pants outward. Maliq stood up and dropped his pants to the floor. He turned and faced the mirror and noticed himself growing as he stroked it up and down. *First the head, then the shaft. Rhythm changing. Fast then slow. Breathing changes. Thoughts of Rain's ass and breasts. Rhythm changing. Slow then fast. Thoughts of Rain riding that thang! Oh shit!* That was all she wrote.
"Whew!" Maliq's love juices were all over his right hand. As he was getting up to go take a shower, his phone rang. *Damn*, he thought. *It's probably Rain.*
"Hello?"
"Hey, Maliq what's up?"
"Nothing *now*," he stated looking down at his deflated dick.

"Huh?"
"Nothing."
"Well, I was just calling to let you know it was a long drive back to Fayetteville, but I made it home safely."
Maliq lived in Douglasville, so he always made it home sooner than I did. He lived closer to the city.
"Anyway, so what were you doing when I called? You sounded a little distracted. Hell, you almost sounded like you just got through getting your groove on."
"Uh, nothing. But I was just about to get into the shower when you called."
"Fine, I can take a hint Maliq. If you need me call me."
"Alright. And the same goes to you, hear?"
"Yep."
"Goodnight Rain."

## Chapter 6
## It's our anniversary

Earlier that evening, Dominic snuck home early to surprise Aaries for their anniversary. Initially, he had to work late, but managed to convince his supervisor to let him go early. As he crept through the back door, he peeked through the house to make sure Aaries was nowhere in sight. The coast was clear. As he turned to close and lock the door, his wife startled him.

"Looking for me?" Aaries questioned in a seductive tone. She stopped Dominic in his tracks with one arm behind his back. He was amazed at how she looked. She had always been beautiful to him, but this time was different. It was special. He was speechless as he took her all in from head to toe. She wore her natural hair in a wild and sexy mane. The same way she suggested that I wear mine. And she spun around to reveal her low cut, backless, red, spaghetti strapped dress with sandals to match. And her make-up was flawless. She never wore too much, just enough to accent her natural beauty.

"You're gorgeous" Dominic said as he walked toward her.

"Thank you baby."

"These are for you Aaries." Behind his back was a bouquet of her favorite flowers…lilies.
She smiled. "They're beautiful."
"Not as beautiful as you are."
"Here, let me go and put…"
Dominic cut her off mid-sentence and gave her a passionate kiss. As they kissed, he towered over her tremendously. Dominic's height would have definitely helped him get closer to the NBA along with his tight game, but he dropped out of college his sophomore year. While they were kissing, Aaries touched the back of his neck and was reminded that he had recently cut his hair low.
"Happy anniversary baby." Her burgundy lipstick was smeared around both of their mouths.
"Happy anniversary," Aaries said smiling.
"Let me go and shower and get cleaned up."
Aaries nodded. "I'll be waiting."

As Dominic was showering, Aaries finished setting the table and decided to use her lilies as the centerpiece and turned the food on simmer. As she was getting the goblets for some wine, Dominic yelled out for her. Aaries went upstairs to see what he wanted.
"Baby, what do you need, I'm trying to finish setting everything up."

He pulled the shower curtain back far enough to reveal his chest and some of his lower torso. "Baby, where's the soap"

"Now, I know you didn't call me up here for some damn soap?"
Dominic was so absolutely spoiled, that once he got into the shower he didn't like to step out until he was finished. He hated the cold air and would freeze. But Aaries didn't mind catering to him, because he took damn good care of her. But this time he had something else on his mind besides the soap. Aaries reached down in the cabinet under the sink and grabbed a fresh bar. She pulled the shower curtain back a little and noticed that her husband was already ready for her. Then they stared each other down and gave each other that look that said…it's on now!!

Aaries took her sandals off and nothing more. At that moment Aaries didn't care about that dress or her hair. She got in the shower with her husband. The water ran down their faces as they began kissing very heavily. Then Dominic picked her up, and she wrapped her legs around his waist and held her arms around his neck. She moaned with every thrust. Although Dominic was ready to climax, he always waited for Aaries. He always made sure that she was taken care of first. When Aaries was ready, she bellowed so loud that it echoed throughout the bathroom. He put her down.
"Oh, shit!" Aaries legs had become weak. All she wanted to do now was go to sleep.

"Yeah, I know the feeling," he said out of breath. As he dried her body off, he kissed her forehead and told her how beautiful she was. Then he picked her up and took her to the bed.
"What are you doing Dominic? I need to go back downstairs and finish setting everything out."
"Baby, we got all night. Come on lie down with me for a minute. I want to give you one of your anniversary gifts."
Aaries smiled. "Ok."

He began to sing *pretty lady* to her, a ballad that he had written a few months back. Although he worked as a security guard, his dreams and aspirations were to make it as a singer. And he had recently been working in the studio on his second c.d. His first one went underground and did pretty well, locally. She smiled in adoration as she listened to him serenade her.
"I wrote that for you."
"It's beautiful, thank you. I love you so much."
"I love you too Mrs. Giles," he smiled. As they lay down, she also took note of how their beautiful skin contrasted - chocolate against butterscotch. That was just one of the beautiful things about being a black woman. We come in so many different flavors - chocolate, mocha, honey, and caramel. She placed her hand on his chest to feel his heartbeat. As she did this, she could also feel her own heartbeat against his body as it

reverberated. Then she realized their hearts were beating at the same time…two hearts, beating as one.

## Chapter 7
## Recollection

One month later:

As Jack waited for his client to meet him at *Lena's Place*, he took notice of the décor of the restaurant. My sister and I wanted it to appear to be somewhat eclectic. There was an oversized aquarium near the rear of the restaurant that one could see upon entrance. It gave the restaurant a new millennium feel. We played music along the lines of Jill Scott, Kem, India Arie, and Floetry - Neo-Soul. The music and décor were modern and hip, yet still appealing to the grown and sexy crowd. It kept them coming back for more than just the food. They wanted ambiance, as well.

There was also a vintage flair to the restaurant. The furniture, chandeliers in the lobby, and the tables and chairs were 1920's vintage style. The furniture sat on beautifully polished hardwood flooring.

Our menu was diverse, as well. The food ranged from catfish and soul food to the best unique seafood dishes you have ever tasted. Whatever you're craving, you could find it at Lena's.

By the way, did I mention Lena's is our family business? Lena is our grandmother from my father's side. She died when Aaries and I were about ten years old. And although Aaries and I went to college, originally we had no intentions of taking over the business. But it worked out anyway. Aaries majored in accounting, and I majored in business administration. Upon graduation, we sat down and decided that it only made sense to use our skills in our own family business, rather than working to help someone else's business thrive.

Just as his server was approaching the table, Jack's cell phone rang.

"Hello?" He motioned for the server to give him a moment with one finger.

"Sure that's fine. Do you know when you would like to reschedule? Alright, just call me when you're ready. Not a problem, I understand. These things happen sometimes. Sure. Will do. Bye."

Jack's client had cancelled their lunch meeting. Jack decided he would stay and order lunch anyway. He hoped our food was good and that this just wasn't some posh restaurant in a pretty package with bad service, horrible food, and a price range to match. He motioned for the server that he was ready to order. His server was a frail looking waif with a close haircut - so close

she was damn near bald. She was one of our newer servers. "You ready to order?"
Jack decided upon the catfish dinner and a white wine spritzer. He decided since he wouldn't be back into the office for the rest of the day, it would be ok to have a tiny little nip. As he was awaiting his meal, he needed to go the restroom. He looked around and noticed it was in the rear, just to the left of the aquarium. As Jack walked to the bathroom, he was still admiring the restaurant. As he approached the bar area, he noticed someone that he thought he had met before. She was beautiful, but her demeanor was different. Her hair was dyed auburn. At first he couldn't put his finger on it, and then he remembered meeting me at the gas station a little while ago. But unbeknownst to Jack, it was Aaries. She was speaking with one of the bartenders when Jack approached her.
"Excuse me pretty lady, how are you?"
She looked him up and down. "No, excuse you," she said matter of factly. That was rude. Didn't you just see us talking?"
"I'm sorry. It's just that when I realized where I remembered you from, I got a little carried away, that's all. I really just wanted to say hello."
"I see. So where am I supposed to know you from?"

"I met you about a month ago at the gas station. Remember? I gave you my card. My name is Jack, and I'm a stock broker."
Jack realized by the look on her face that she didn't remember him.
"You're Rain right?"
Aaries was used to being mistaken for me and vice versa, but this time the thought hadn't occurred to her. She shot Jack a faint smile.
"No, I'm not Rain. Hold on and I'll get her for you." Jack had a puzzled look on his face. *Damn, if she's not interested all she had to do is just say so.*

When Aaries and I both walked in his direction, he was taken aback. When we both approached the bar area, Aaries resumed her business with the bartender. Honestly at first I didn't remember him. Then as we began to talk, he jogged my memory.
"...right it was about a month ago at the gas station," Jack said. I thought you would have called, so we could go out for a drink or something."
"I have just been so busy Jack." As I stood next to him I could smell his cologne - *Bora Bora* for men. Damn, he smelled good.
"Well, how about tonight Rain? We could go to the Atlantic Station and just talk."

I figured what the hell. One drink won't hurt. And if we don't click I just won't go out with him anymore. Besides, he looks harmless enough anyway. We decided to meet each other there at seven o'clock.

.

## Chapter 8
## The date

Later that evening, I agreed to meet Jack at a quaint little spot inside the Atlantic Station. I figured since I was just getting to know him that I'd keep it casual. I decided to wear a white linen, capri pants suit and a pair of tan wedges. And I sported a tan head wrap that revealed a bevy of twists sticking out of the top and draping down like a waterfall. My makeup was simple with only a little mascara and just a hint of color on my lips. After all, I already possessed a natural beauty that most women only dream of. A little makeup only enhanced my naturalness.

After waiting awhile, I had become increasingly irritated. Jack was late. I mean, at best, I had probably only been waiting for ten or fifteen minutes, but that's not the point. Time waits for no one. Who does he think he is anyway? I mean after sweating me a couple of times, I finally agree to go out with him and he's late. At that very moment, I had decided to leave, and Jack showed up.

"Going somewhere?"

Jack stood there grinning with a dozen red roses. For a second, I had forgotten all about his tardiness.

"These are for you. That's the reason I'm late. Sorry."

I really wanted to give him a hard time, but he softened me with the flowers. All I could do was take in their fragrance and smile.

"Thank you, they're beautiful." I quickly gave Jack a friendly hug.

As Jack sat down, the server arrived.

"Are you two ready to order?"

I took the liberty of answering.

"Actually, I think I'm just going to have some dessert," I said as I licked my lips.

"This looks good," I told her as I pointed to a picture on the menu.

"Good choice ma'am. That's the plain cheesecake. Is that what you would like?"

"Yes, and a french vanilla cappuccino, as well."

The server nodded, then looked in Jack's direction.

"And for you sir?"

Jack was smiling. He was just elated to be in my presence.

"You know, I'll have the same," he said handing the menu to the server.

"Very well. I'll be back shortly."

After the server left, we sort of sat in silence momentarily. Jack decided to break the ice.
"You look lovely."
"Thank you. You look nice too. And it looks like we had the same idea with the linen."
"Yeah, it's a nice change, but...well I don't get a chance to dress down much, because I'm always working. So I'm always in a stuffy suit."
"Oh, really? So then you don't get out much? I mean as far as dating is concerned?" I wanted to know what his story was. *A good-looking man like that surely has women doting over him.*

Jack explained that he really didn't do much and that he was a creature of habit. Everyday it was the same thing pretty much - hit the gym, go to work and come home.

Still bedazzled that he was sitting across from the most beautiful woman he had ever laid eyes on, Jack wanted to know more about me; for some reason, he thought I was mysterious. I could see his wheels turning and I could tell he wanted to ask me a lot of questions. So, I decided to beat him to the punch. I asked him to tell me more about himself.
"Not much to tell, but what would you like to know?"
"You know. How old you are, where are you from? Just small talk..."

I was a headstrong woman and I didn't believe in giving too much information too soon. I also knew how to flip the script. So I decided to dig into his psyche.

Jack smiled. He understood what I was doing and it was fine with him. He didn't mind humoring me.

"Well, I'm from right here in the 'A' as we call it, thirty-five, single with no children, and I'm gainfully employed. Does that sum up what you were wanting to hear?"

I laughed.

"Yes, that will do for now. But you make everything so simple and uncomplicated. What gives?"

"What do you mean?" Jack had a peculiar look on his face."

"Thirty-five, single with no kids, and successful. In Atlanta, you're a catch. So why aren't you with a woman yet? Are you gay or one of the DL brothas?"

I'm pretty sure I pissed him off with that question. But he understood where I was coming from, with HIV and AIDS out there. One couldn't be too careful. Besides, it's not as if a man was going to admit to that anyway.

"No. Neither one," he said matter of factly in a more serious tone.

"I'm sorry, I wasn't trying to offend you, but hey this is Atlanta. And the ratio is twenty women to every man. So when you said you were thirty-five and single I just thought..."

Jack cut me off mid-sentence.

"It's ok. I know this is the black gay capitol, but I swing one way. But why don't you tell me a little about you." Jack wanted to change the subject.

I still wanted to know some more about him, but I indulged him.

"Well, I'm twenty-nine." "You already know I have a twin."

Jack nodded and smiled.

"My sister and I own Lena's. My grandmother started it several years ago when it was just a smoked meats house. In fact, she used to call it Lena's house of smoked meats."

"So that's you all's specialty then, huh?" Jack inquired.

"Well, it was years ago. My family is from St. Louis. When they moved here, they realized it was a unique idea for Atlanta. So they decided on smoked meats and barbecue. And my Dad patented a special sauce just for the restaurant. My sister and I just decided when we took over that we wanted to create a more versatile menu. So we still have our smoked meats and BBQ section, but we also expanded on the menu."

"I see. So you're intelligent as you are beautiful."
I gave a faint smile. I was confident and was used to getting compliments. And because my father was around, I didn't need to squirm and giggle every time a man paid me a compliment.
"Thank you Jack."
Jack wanted to get a little more personal.
"So, what about a man in your life? I find it hard to believe that no one has stolen your heart."
I explained to Jack that I wasn't looking for a relationship, but at the same time if love found me that that is something that I would embrace wholeheartedly. I guess some people would have considered what I do as being a player but I call it, exploring my options.
Jack nodded his head, but I could tell he didn't like what he heard. But as long as I'm being honest with him, he can't ever say I didn't keep it real with him.
Throughout the conversation and unbeknownst to me he was already imagining kissing and making love to me. He had already begun to think of me as his woman.

"So how about you Jack? What do you want?"
"The same thing."
"You're just looking for that ideal quality woman, right?"
"Yep."

We were still engaged in conversation when my cell phone rang.
"Excuse me Jack."
"Oh, by all means," he smiled.
I hurriedly rummaged through my purse. When I finally found it, I saw it was Maliq calling.
Jack pretended to be preoccupied with other things, but he was really eavesdropping.
"Hey Maliq."
As soon as Jack heard me mention a man's name, his blood boiled. *Who in the hell is Maliq? Better be a damn relative for her sake.* As he continued to listen, the server brought our cake and cappuccino to the table.
"What? When? Ok, no problem. You know I gotcha back. Ok. I don't want to be rude, but I'm out with a friend right now, so I'm going to have to call you later. Atlantic Station…um-hmm. Alright. We'll talk later."
I let out a small chuckle, which led Jack to believe that Maliq must've asked me a question about him. Plus I had begun to give yes and no answers. He knew what was up.
"I'm sorry Jack. That was my best friend Maliq. He needed to talk to me about something important."
*This shit is going to cease real quick. I'm going to see to that. And what self respecting woman has a man for a best friend.*

"That's alright. I understand. After all you said you're best friends, right?"
Rain smiled and nodded.
*I will put an end to this shit*, Jack thought. Rain is mine!

# Chapter 9
# Infatuation

When Jack got home, all he could do was think about me. He wanted to call, but he didn't want to seem too eager. But he just couldn't resist. I was just about to jump into the shower when my cell rang. When I picked up the phone, I guess he could hear the hesitancy in my voice to speak with him. After all, it had only been about an hour since we had seen each other. Jack explained that he wasn't calling to bug me; he simply wanted to make sure I made it home. I felt better about the call after that.

After we spoke, Jack immediately jumped on the computer. Once he logged on, he decided to "google" me. He used some sort of people finder website that dug into my personal business. And the more one was willing to pay, the more information one could get. Of course, he decided to get the most expensive one to get an extensive background check on me. It even gave him my unlisted home phone number. Once again, he couldn't resist. He blocked his home number and began dialing my home phone.

When I picked up, I got dead silence. I just figured someone got the wrong number and was too embarrassed to say so or someone was playing on my phone.

Jack began to imagine us as a married couple with kids.
*Yeah, you're mine. And nothing and no one is going to stand in our way Rain. I'll see to that. And getting rid of this Maliq character is going to be the first step*, he thought as he took his letter opener and stabbed the arm of his couch cushion.

## Chapter 10
## Theory

Just as I was about to lie down for the night, Aaries called. She called to find out how my date with Jack went. I told her overall it went well, nothing to boast about though. He's got money and good looks, but so far there isn't much more to him. I guess you could say he's still in the "friend zone".

"Well, what about Maliq," she asked me.

"What about Maliq, Aaries?"

"Is he still in the friend zone, too?"

I rolled my eyes. Aaries was forever trying to hook Maliq and I up with each other.

"I keep telling you, we're best friends and will remain that way."

"Um-hmm, whatever you say little sis. The best marriages start from being best friends."

"Even if we weren't best friends, he's not my type. I like dark men. Maliq is just a little darker than me. I like suit and tie men. Maliq walks around in jeans all the time. I like professional men. Maliq is an electrician. So, you see there are too many differences."

"Rain I keep telling you that you need a little thug passion in your life."
"Aaries, you got your nerve anyway. You talk like Dominic is still in the streets."
"No, he's not anymore. But I like to think of him as an educated thug. He got a little college under his belt, so he's got some book smarts. But he's a hustler at the same time; and he knows how to get back into the streets to make money legitimately."

Dominic at one time was a jack-of-all-trades. He did everything under the sun from boosting to street pharmacy. But after a while, he got tired of it. He matured and became legit.
Call waiting interrupted our conversation. It was Maliq. I simply told Aaries I had to take the call, I didn't tell her it was Maliq; otherwise I would not have heard the end of it.

Maliq was simply calling to finish our conversation from earlier this evening. He wanted to tell me he was taking his ex-wife to court and needed me as a character witness.

Then he started asking me about the date with Jack.
"Damn, everybody's getting in my business today."
"What are you talking about?"
I told him first Aaries was all up in my business and now him. But I didn't mind. After all, he is my best friend; and we told each other practically

everything. I told him things about men and me; and likewise, he told me things about him and women. And we gave each other advice, nothing more, nothing less.

# Chapter 11
# Baby who? Baby what?

As Dominic gave his wife a massage, his mind grew heavy with thoughts. He had wanted them to start a family as soon as they got married. Aaries wasn't trying to hear that. She told him that she wanted to wait a few years before starting a family, anyway.

"Oh, baby that feels so good," she moaned. He was kneading her back. She had been working out the last few weeks and her muscles were tight. When something was on Dominic's mind, he had to just come on out with it.

"You know babe, I think our marriage is perfect except for one thing."

"What D?"

"A baby."

He immediately felt her body tense up.

"What's wrong? I feel you tensing all up?"

She turned over to face him. "What's wrong is the fact that we've discussed this several times D. I told you I'm not ready and I don't want to start a family for a while."

"But you haven't given me a good enough reason not to start one, other than the fact that you're not ready. Is there anything wrong with me being in love with my wife and wanting a baby? The deepest connection between two people is bringing life into this world. That's stronger than marriage."

At times, when Dominic spoke, he got all philosophical on her and deep.

"I didn't say there was anything wrong with that. I'm just saying with me and where I am at this point in my life…it's not gonna happen. Point blank."

"Oh. You act like you're still single - like you're the only one in this relationship. That's selfish Aaries."

"Look let's just drop this, D."

Dominic paused for a moment. "Oh don't worry. I won't bring it up again anytime soon."

Aaries thought the way he said that was strange. It was almost as if there was something that she didn't know about.

This seemed to be the only thing that they argued about; and it had begun to put a serious strain on their relationship.

## Chapter 12
## New Orleans

It had been a couple of weeks since I had seen Jack. This was fine with me and even better for his sake. After our first date, I worried for a second. I thought he was going to turn out to be one of those stalker types, especially when he called me later on the same night. But that was not the case. He actually turned out to be someone whom I thought I might become involved with.

Even though we hadn't seen each other since our first date, we talked quite a bit. I was able to get to know him pretty well over the phone and through e-mails. Jack is an interesting man. Aside from being fine, he's kind, sweet and generous. In fact he was so generous, he asked me to accompany him overnight to New Orleans for a night of some great seafood and jazz. Quite honestly, even though I really liked him, I didn't feel comfortable going out of town with him. But after thinking about the food and the music, I decided to go. After all, we didn't have to stay in the same hotel room. It was perfect, and I wouldn't be away from the restaurant that long.

The next Sunday afternoon when we arrived to New Orleans, it was a little on the cool side. But Jack and I decided to make the best of it and have a great time. Indeed that is what we did. Once we deplaned, Jack got a rental car. After we both checked into our hotel rooms, we decided to just walk up and down the French Quarters and shop. We had a ball, just laughing and talking. And despite the crisp weather, we saw a few of those gypsy fortune-tellers. And just for fun, we both decided to see what our fortune entailed. Benoit is the fortune-teller that told me my fortune. He was white with long scraggly hair. He was all bundled up in dirty gloves and a greasy skullcap. If you ask me, he looked more like a functioning crack head getting his hustle on to get that next hit. He told me that I was going to be married after a short time; and that I was going to have four children. Jack and I thought it was hilarious and just laughed. When he read Jack his fortune, it was sort of gloomy. He told Jack that he was going to live a short life, but he would have the love of his life with no children. Strangely, enough Jack just smiled. After that, we paid Benoit, the fortune-teller, his five dollars each.

After that we were famished and decided to go eat. Jack told me about this little hole in the wall called *Acme Oyster House*. He said they have the best Creole food in New Orleans. By this time, it was about four o'clock in the afternoon. Jack suggested that we go back to our hotel rooms and get changed. He said he wanted to go straight to the quaint little jazz place after we ate. I told him I'd be ready in forty minutes, but that turned into an hour and a half. Jack didn't seem to be upset, though. He said it wasn't a problem and for me to call his room when I was done, so he could meet me down in the lobby. In fact, he was so cool that he seemed to be ok with anything I said or did.

One of the reasons it took me so long was because I decided to call Aaries to let her know I was ok; and that I was having a good time. Once we get on the phone, it's hard for us to talk for only five minutes. I think we were on the phone for at least twenty minutes. Once she and I hung up, I ran around that hotel room like a chicken with her head cut off. I was trying to hurry since I knew Jack was waiting on me.

I decided upon something simple to wear, a simple black dress. A woman could never go wrong with a simple black dress. It was a v-neck, sexy, slinky dress that sat slightly above the knees. All I had to do was add my chandelier diamond earrings and a necklace to match. The accessories set the whole thing off. Then I put my makeup on. Tonight I wanted to be ultra sexy. When I was little, my mom would refer to this as "being fast". I applied liquid to powder foundation, eye shadow, eyeliner, mascara, and finally a sexy plum lipstick. And I had decided to pin my hair up to reveal my neckline.

Jack was waiting for me in the lobby. When the elevator door opened and I walked out, Jack was flabbergasted and so was I. Jack was smoking a cigarette. And we were probably at one of the last hotels that still allowed inside smoking. I guess they figured their guests paid enough to do whatever they wanted, which included smoking. Jack smiled and walked up to me.

"You look beautiful, Rain," he said as he kissed me on the cheek.

"Thanks, so do you. But tell me, what's with the cigarette? I've never seen you smoke and you've never told me you smoked," I said displeasingly. "Oh, this? Well, the only time I smoke is when I'm nervous or I'm celebrating." "So which one are you Jack?" "Celebrating, of course. I mean, I'm going out with a beautiful woman tonight. It's not every day that I get to do this, so why not celebrate," he said very charmingly. "But I can see that it bothers you, so I won't do it again," he said as he put the cigarette out in the ashtray. "Thank you," I told him with a quick peck on the cheek.

That made me smile and he did look good. He had on a black suit and a pair of Stacy Adams. And he smelled good, too. This brotha was setting it out and it made me want to drop my panties. But then again, maybe it was a combination of him and the fact that I hadn't had sex in over six months. Shit, I better be careful or it could be on and poppin' tonight. And I can't let that happen, especially since I have a three-month rule. I have a dresser-drawer full of bedroom tools that help me along. The bullet and the venus-penis give a whole new meaning to abstinence, but ain't nothin' like some real D-I-C-K.

The rest of the night was absolutely wonderful. I ate well that night. I decided upon a sample platter that had a little bit of everything on it. It consisted of gumbo, red beans and rice, smoked sausage and jambalaya. Jack had decided upon the catfish and oysters platter.

After we ate, we took in some old school bluesy-jazz. Then Jack walked me up to my hotel room, which was two floors up from his. I told him I had a good time and then he kissed me on the cheek again. As he did that, the wine I drank at the jazz club got to talking to me; and I turned my head and gave him a long, deep, sensuous kiss. He pulled me to him and I noticed that he was hard. And when I started to get wet, I decided it was time for me to go inside my room and go to sleep, before I got into trouble.

## Chapter 13
## Chit chat

On the flight home the next morning, while everyone else was eating milk and cereal, I was tearing up a shrimp po-boy. Jack asked me last night before going into my room if there was anything he could get me. The food that evening was so good; and I was so greedy. I just had to have another shrimp po-boy. It was very late, but the restaurant was still open. This was one of the beauties of New Orleans. You could enjoy the same things at night that you did during the day. Anyway, when he brought it to me, I kept it wrapped up in the bag it came in and put it in the mini-fridge in my room. On the plane, I had the flight attendants to zap it in the microwave for me.

The flight was nice and short, but long enough to give Jack and I some time to talk and enjoy each other some more. It seemed as if we talked about everything under the sun during that hour and a half flight. He told me that this was the best birthday he had ever had. "Jack, why didn't you tell me it was your birthday?"
He shrugged his shoulders. "I don't know. I really don't discuss it or make a big deal out of it.

But let's change the subject." I knew there was a story there, but I didn't want to push.

We started talking about family and what we did after graduation. At that time, I was eager to get out of Atlanta and have a little freedom away from my parents. But Aaries and I always had to be together. We weren't those twins that couldn't stand each other. Anyway, we were far enough away from Atlanta, but not too far. We could still drive home from school when we wanted to. We attended University of North Carolina at Chapel Hill. Jack said he went to Tuskegee. I learned quite a bit about him. He said that he went to Tuskegee partially to spite his parents. They wanted him to go to an Ivy League school. But because Jack went to a private school, which was predominantly white, he wanted to get a chance to enjoy being around his people. His parents finally relented and he was able to attend Tuskegee University on a full scholarship.

Jack said although he enjoyed it, he stood out like a sore thumb. They called him the black white-boy. His description reminded me of Braxton from the Jamie Foxx show – a total square.

And interestingly enough, neither one of us had decided to pledge. I for one thought that sororities were nothing more than immature cliques. I didn't have time for that. Although, there were some people that kept a level head involving the organizations, most did not. Most tend to let it consume them. And they were all so predictable. First came the corny license plates and the attitude followed. It just seemed, for most, that it was their life in whole, rather than allowing it to just be *a part* of one's life.

Jack said he wanted to belong to a fraternity but none of them wanted him. And he wanted to do it the traditional way. He didn't just want to pay dues and belong. He wanted to be accepted and wanted everything that came along with pledging. When that didn't happen, he got a job his senior year as an accountant and fell in love with number crunching. That's how he got involved with stocks and other investments.

He also told me that he was an only child and he's only had three serious relationships. And he's very eager to get married and start a family. That's where Jack and I differ. I have no expectations. I go out with intentions on having a good time and focusing on good company. If later it turns into something else, then so be it; but I'm not trying to force anything.

Once we touched down into Hartsfield-Jackson International Airport, we both gave each other a hug and a quick peck on the lips and told one another how much we enjoyed each other's company. Then we went our separate ways.

# Chapter 14
# Stop lyin'

Aaries had decided to take off of work early to go spend time with her fine husband. When she got home, she was disappointed that Dominic had not yet made it home. Then she thought, maybe he was just running late. Once she thought about it, that actually worked out better for her. It gave her time to really set it out for her man. She took a quick shower and then put on the sexiest lingerie she could find from her collection. She put on a leather baby doll with matching leather panties and three-inch heels. And she put her hair up in a sexy, bushy ponytail.

After about an hour or so, he still had not shown up. Aaries wanted to be sexy, but it was damn near winter and she was starting to get cold. She draped herself in her bathrobe and watched TV. while she awaited Dominic.

A few hours later, she heard Dominic pull into the garage. At first she wanted to meet him at the door in her attire, but then she decided to wait until Dominic walked into the bedroom.

When Dominic walked into the room, it was obvious that Aaries didn't have anything on her mind but getting straight-freaky-deaky..getting down and dirty. Aaries was on their bed rubbing her titties with one hand and the other hand was under her panties rubbing her clit.

"Damn!" That was all he could say when he walked in the room.

"Hi honey," she said in a seductive tone.

Dominic smiled. "Baby, what are you doing?"

"What does it look like," Aaries said as she stood up to kiss her husband. She made Dominic lick the same fingers she used to rub herself.

When she walked up to him, she kissed him long and deep. She put her hands in his pants and rubbed him until he became rigid.

"Baby, I just came home to shower and change. I'm supposed to be meeting Barren and them up at the studio."

Barren was his best friend. They used to run together in the streets and now Barren owns his own recording studio and helps produce local talent.

"Oh really? I bet I can change your mind." As she began to kiss him on the neck, she noticed he smelled like women's perfume. And the scent was not her own. She immediately frowned up and took a step back.

"Where have you been Dominic? And why did it take you so long to get home?"

When Aaries questioned him, he immediately looked away.

"I had to work late that's all."
Aaries stared at him suspiciously. "Um-hmm. Why do you smell like perfume? Who were you all hugged up with Dominic?"
"Just a female co-worker that I haven't seen in a while…I just gave her an innocent hug."
Aaries knew he was lying. He could never look her straight in the eye when he was lying. Plus he was behaving rather nervously.
"Ok, I'm gonna ask you this again. This time, you might wanna try telling me the truth Dominic."
"I don't appreciate you accusing me of something. Now I'm gonna repeat myself and that's the last time I'm gonna mention it. I gave my co-worker a hug and that's it. I stayed late, because I worked a couple hours overtime. Now, if you're gonna start accusing me of shit, then maybe we shouldn't be married."
Aaries rolled her eyes at him. "Excuse you?"
"I'm just saying…we're married. And you're supposed to trust me. If we don't have trust Babe, we don't have anything."

Aaries couldn't stand it. She knew he was lying and blowing a bunch of smoke up her ass. She wasn't sure how to handle it, because she never had to go through anything like that with him, not even when they were dating. She was pissed. She threw on her robe and stormed out of the room.

Dominic called after her. "Wait a minute, I thought you wanted to get your freak on?"
By this time, she was half way down the stairs. She yelled back up to him.
"Nope, never mind. You go on and handle your business at the studio."

Dominic knew that she was pissed. He also knew that she could tell when he was lying. He didn't mean to lie to her, but he felt like he was trying to protect her. The reason why he was late getting home was because he ran into his ex-girlfriend Reah. He didn't cheat on Aaries. He would never do that. He loved and respected her too much.

Reah had some news for him. She told him that her five-year-old daughter was also his daughter. Of course he was shocked, especially after all this time. He asked her why she waited so long to tell him. Reah claimed that after they broke up she was so devastated that she moved back home to Texas. But now all of a sudden, she felt it was only right for her child to meet her father. Dominic was upset. Not because he thought he had a child, but because she waited so long to tell him. Dominic told Reah that he wanted them to get a paternity test done before he met his "daughter". She agreed and he gave her his cell phone number.

He wasn't planning on telling Aaries until he was absolutely sure. He didn't want to upset her.

## Chapter 15
## Happy New Year!

The holidays came and went without a hitch. And tonight was New Year's Eve. Aaries and I decided that we would do something special this year, and turn the restaurant into a club for one night. It sure couldn't hurt business. We planned on decorating and rearranging the tables. We would keep the kitchen open for finger foods only. Our cover charge would only be twenty dollars, while everyone else was charging thirty and up, depending on the venue. It was not a bad price considering we were able to get Chante Moore, Musiq Soulchild, and Donell Jones to perform.

I decided, since Jack and I had started to become closer, to invite him to come along tonight. Besides, Aaries and Maliq were anxious to meet him anyway.

Aaries and I got there first around eight o'clock just to make sure that everything was to our liking. The crowd wouldn't start pouring in until closer to ten o'clock or so.

Once people started to arrive, it was like a fashion show. Women were trying to out-do other women, with who could look the most hoochiefied. Men were trying to out-do each other by seeing who had the most ice. But for the most part, the majority of the crowd was pretty classy. …Evening gowns, cocktail dresses and tuxedos. I had decided upon a long, sparkly, green, backless dress with spaghetti straps and a high split. I also pressed my hair out and wore it straight. Aaries wore an all black short dress that went to her knees; and he wore her hair pinned up in a bun. Dominic and Maliq both wore sports coats.

By the time Jack rolled into the restaurant it was 11:22pm. When I saw him, I immediately walked up to him and gave him a hug. I enjoyed seeing him; and I was elated that he could make it.

I introduced him to the whole gang. I noticed he seemed cool with everyone until I got to Maliq. He shook his hand, but seemed to be somewhat aloof and standoffish. He appeared to have a distrustful look in his eyes. And he looked him up and down, too, almost as if he was sizing up Maliq.

Jack pulled me on the dance floor and much to my surprise, he knew how to get his groove on. But I knew that was more for Maliq. He was sending him a message. I swear…men and their egos.

After that, we danced several songs and when it was ten minutes 'til midnight, I had the servers pass out complimentary glasses of champagne. Aaries and I decided to let Dominic open up the show to help promote one of the new songs he had written. He also did the emceeing for the rest of the night, as well. Musiq Soulchild was up first. Once the clock struck midnight, we all got together at our table to toast each other. But before Dominic went back to emceeing, the newlyweds toasted each other and kissed like there was no tomorrow. Then Maliq toasted me, simply as a friend and gave me a kiss on the cheek. Jack was fuming. He decided to "one up" Maliq. He toasted me and then gave me the deepest kiss. I was a little taken back, especially since I'm not very fond of public affection. My sister, Dominic, and Maliq all looked at each other. They were as shocked as I was that Jack had done that. We all sat in an uncomfortable silence until we were saved by the band. Musiq Soulchild had just finished his set, and the crowd went wild. Dominic almost forgot that he was doing the emceeing, so he had to run up to the microphone. Chante Moore was up next.

Although, Maliq didn't come with a date, he didn't have a problem with women approaching him. They had their eyes on him and were coming out of the woodworks left and right. In fact, one of those women had asked him to dance. He obliged her. Shortly after that, Jack excused himself to the restroom leaving Aaries and I at the table alone.

As soon as Jack left, she gave me her opinion of him. And she was going to do that whether I liked it or not.

"I don't like him, Rain. There's just something about him that I can't put my finger on."

I rolled my eyes at her. "So how can you say you don't like Jack, when you can't even figure out what it is that bothers you about him?"

Aaries knew I was right and she shrugged her shoulders. Aaries was the type that no matter if she was wrong, she was still right.

"Well, it doesn't matter anyway. I'm your sister and I know *who's* good for you. And it ain't him."

"Well, whatever, he's kind, sweet, and attentive to my needs. What more could I ask for? Besides, once he met you guys, he tried to strike up conversations with you and Dominic, but you two acted like he had the bubonic plague or something."

Aaries immediately switched the focus onto Maliq. "Well, like I said before, I know what type of man you need, and he ain't it. But I tell you this; Maliq has been staring at you all night, even now since he's been dancing with that woman. That man is in love with you, I can see it in his eyes. You can't hide that."

Even though I wouldn't admit it to my sister, I was beginning to wonder if she was at least partially right. I definitely didn't think that Maliq was in love me. Aaries was just seeing what she wanted to see. But also, I had noticed that I caught Maliq a few times looking at me. And what do you know, I glance over to see if Maliq is looking at me and low and behold, there he was.

After a few songs I noticed that Jack was taking a long time in the bathroom. I decided to check on him. Maybe he was sick or something. I was surprised to see him in our office where Aaries kept our accounting. Apparently, she had not locked the door before we opened up for the night.

"What are you doing?"

I startled Jack. He jumped.

"Oh, I was just coming from the bathroom and I just thought I'd take a detour. The door was open. I didn't bother anything. I just wanted to take a look around."

I was pissed off. Somehow I thought he was snooping and I didn't like that. I didn't believe a word he said.

"Well this is off limits to anyone that doesn't work here, so come on out."

He must have sensed that what he told me didn't set well with me and tried to get back into my good graces.
"I'm sorry Rain, it won't happen again." He kissed my hand as he spoke to me.
I decided, what the hell, it's New Years Eve and I let it go. As we walked back out, Chante was closing up with one of my favorites, from her first album, 'Loves taken over'.

Soon Donell Jones came out and began performing from his newest cd, J*ourney of a Gemini.* He sang *special girl.* Maliq saw Jack and I walking back to the table and excused himself from the woman he was dancing with. He wanted to dance with me. Even though Jack and I weren't a couple per se, I didn't want him to think I was disrespecting him.
"You don't mind do you Jack?"
He looked kind of surprised, but he seemed to play it off well. "Nah, it's cool, go ahead."

When Maliq and I danced it seemed almost magical. It felt so right to be in his arms like this. I couldn't understand for the life of me why I was feeling this way about my best friend. He ran his thumb down my spine and all I felt were shivers. Our faces were on the side of each other and I could feel him smelling my hair. Then all of a sudden, Maliq felt the need to talk during the song.

"So what's up with you and dude?"
"Nothing. We're just friends."
Maliq looked me in my eyes. "Friends with benefits?"
"No. You remember I told you a while back that I was seeing him and I went off to New Orleans with him?"
It was weird talking to Maliq like this; it almost seemed as if he were jealous. Normally, when we talk to each other about our relationships with other people, its way less serious than the conversation we were having now. Hell, sometimes we even give each other advice. I almost felt guilty that I was talking to Maliq about another man.
"Yeah, well just be careful," he told me. "He thinks he's more than just your friend, trust me. I'm a man and I know what I'm talking about."
I simply nodded my head. When we were done dancing it was almost time to shut everything down and I looked around for Jack, but he was nowhere in sight. I thought he went to the bathroom again. Aaries was at the table and I decided to ask her.
"Where's Jack?"
"He dipped."
"What? When did he do that?"
"While you two were dancing, he just jumped up and said he had to go."

"Well, I hope he wasn't upset, but I did ask him about dancing with Maliq first. He said he did not mind." But then again, he is a man and their egos would never allow them to admit to any insecurity, especially where there is another man involved. Aaries just shrugged her shoulders; she could care less anyway. Then I decided to call Jack on his cell phone and I simply got voicemail. I decided to wait until I got home to give him another call.

# Chapter 16
## Green eyed monster

Jack was furious! He couldn't believe I had asked him if he minded if I danced with Maliq. And then to top that off, he saw the chemistry between the two of us. I guess we couldn't hide that. Not only could he see it in our eyes, but our body language spoke loud and clear as well. He felt disrespected and decided to leave. He turned his cell phone off so he could avoid my calls for the time being.

It was about eleven o'clock the next morning when he decided he felt like being bothered with me. But this time he'd have to reach out to me. I wasn't about to kiss any ass. After all, I had left a message on his voicemail that I'm sure he got long before now. Besides, he needed to stop acting so immature. If he was uncomfortable with Maliq and I dancing, he should've spoke up. Some wise person once said, a closed mouth doesn't get fed.

I decided to answer the phone nonchalantly.

"Hello?"

"Rain, hi. It's me Jack."

"Yeah, I know who it is. What's up?"

Jack must've sensed that I was not in the mood for games, because he got right to the purpose of this call.
"I just want to let you know that I enjoyed your company last night. I really had a good night."
"Really? I sure couldn't tell, especially the way you did that disappearing Cinderella act."
"That's the reason I'm calling. I wanted to apologize for that. I was a little upset. I didn't appreciate your friend trying to show me up like that. After all I came as your date and Maliq should have brought a date with him, so he wouldn't feel so lonely."
"Yeah, well next time, you just need to speak up and say how you really feel."
"Alright, well since we're being so honest Rain, I must say that I don't like you hanging around Maliq. He's got a thing for you.

He really had his nerve telling me some shit like this. I've known Maliq since junior high school and I've known Jack a mere few months and now he's trying to regulate some shit. I don't think so!
"First of all, he's my best friend, Jack. I told you that. Secondly, there has never been and never will be any involvement with each other. And lastly, remember that just because we're seeing each other, doesn't mean that you can tell me what to do. Furthermore, if I want to see someone

else I can do that, too. I don't need your "permission" and you are *not* my man."

Jack was stunned. He didn't really know what to make of that, nor did he know what else to say. Then all of a sudden it just seemed as if he had a Jekyll and Hyde thing going on. I thought he had bumped his head or something, because he just flipped out.

"I know I'm not your man, 'cause if I was that sure as hell wouldn't be going on. And common sense would tell you not to ask me if another man could dance with you. It's just disrespectful. Not to mention that he was all over you and the two of you were hanging all over each other. I mean the way you were carrying on, I thought you might get a room for the night. And as far as I know, you probably did."

Now who was flabbergasted?

"Jack, lose my number and go to hell!" I slammed my cell phone shut.

## Chapter 17
## Take a hint

Several hours later, Jack was still blowing my phone up. It was really beginning to piss me off. He left two messages, apologizing and then I just cut my phone off. But the minute I turn my cell back on, he was calling again. I couldn't even make an outgoing call, because he was calling so much. It was ridiculous!

And Jack became so enraged that it triggered some serious emotions stemming from his early childhood. He thought about several things. One of the first memories was around his seventh or eighth birthday. Jack recalled several birthdays in which his mother refused to get him a cake. Something so simple and enjoyable for a child to partake in; and his parents wouldn't do that for him. Jack even remembers begging his mother in particular for a party or at least a birthday cake. He was about eight at the time.

"Please mommy," he pleaded to her as he hugged at her waist. "I promise to be extra good."

"Jackie, now you know your mother doesn't have time for such trivial things," she said as she pried his hands from her waist. She never liked to be kissed, touched or give out any affection for that matter. "Besides, your father and I are trying our best to teach you how to be a man, not a kid. And what have I told you about calling me mommy? Call me Vivian, do you understand?"

"Yes, ma'am," he said dribbling and wallowing with tears forming in his eyes. Then he looked over at his father who was sitting on the sofa reading his newspaper. Jack was not only looking for approval but he was also hoping for a different answer from his Dad. His father felt Jack's eyes on him and it made him look from underneath his glasses and put his paper down on the coffee table. "Well, don't look at me. You know better Jack. Your mother makes all the decisions."

Jack was so upset by this that he went to his room and cried his eyes out for what seemed like eternity. Needless to say, as a result, Jack spent most of his adult life looking for his "mother figure", and trying to force women to love him. Jack's mother always seemed to be cold and push him away. She never really wanted a child. She was upset when she discovered that she was pregnant with Jack. Jack's mother got her tubes tied after Jack was born. Jack's dad was indifferent and simply a puppet for his wife Vivian.

Another memory caught Jack. It was around age eleven or twelve. He remembered wanting love and affection from his mother so much, that he put a little household cleaner in her scotch. Jack was always intelligent and a scholar. He read a lot and as a result, learned a lot about chemicals, especially since his parents wanted him to be a doctor. One thing he knew was that the chemicals in the cleanser was not enough to kill her, but just enough to make her really sick – at least sick enough for one week of bed rest. This would allow Jack to take care of his mother. All he wanted to do was wait on her with food and drink; and he hoped that she would praise him, thank him, hug him, and kiss him all over in return. Jack desperately wanted her attention.

Jack snapped out of it and grabbed his phone to call my cell again. Once again, he was calling so much I could barely make an outgoing call. All I was trying to do was call Maliq to let him know I was on my way to his house. He had invited several people over for dinner. This was his first New Years away from his son Jaden. He knew he would probably be lonely, so rather than be alone he told us to come over and we could eat and watch football. Personally, I was more of a basketball fan than anything else, but at least it was something to do; plus I get to chill at my homey's house.

Since Jack couldn't take a hint, I decided to use my home phone. I let Maliq know that we were

on our way over. I had decided to ride with Aaries and Dominic. As I was waiting on them to drive down the street to pick me up, Jack called me yet again. This time I was so exasperated I flipped open my phone just to cuss him out. I didn't give him a chance to say a word.
"Look you crazy son of a bitch, I'm only going to tell you this one more time. When I said lose my number, I meant it. So stop calling me! Or maybe you'd understand me better if I call the fucking police huh?"
Again I immediately hung up the phone without giving Jack a chance to respond. And I hated cussing, it was so unnecessary most of the time, but he had brought out the worst in me, I guess. As soon as I hung up on him, Aaries and D had pulled up in their new H2. That had to be the ugliest vehicle I had ever seen - an accessorized army tank with a fresh coat of paint and a high ass price tag. Who knew?

■■■■■■■■■■■■■■■■■■■■■■■■■■■■■■■■■■■■■■■■■■■■■■■■

Jack was going crazy at his house. He was throwing things around his house and punching walls. He had upset himself so much that he had almost begun to cry. He had been calling me for the last few hours only to get my voicemail. He had left at least two messages.

*"I'm so sorry Rain. Please forgive me. You have every right to be mad at me. You don't understand all I want to do is love you. I need you. Just give me the chance and you'll see what a wonderful man I can be to you.*

I deleted it and listened to the second message.

*I didn't mean those nasty things I said to you. I was just upset. I thought that we had made a connection and that we were getting closer. Look if you would just at least talk to me and listen to my point of view, maybe you could understand where I am coming from. I promise not to call you until you are ready and I will at least give you some cool-off time."*

After I cussed him out, he decided that he would pay me a visit. And since he had already googled me, he printed the directions off of the internet. Luckily for him, I wasn't home. Once again he thought I was ignoring him, because my car was simply parked right outside the garage. Jack even walked around the side and back of the house to see if he could peek inside. Finally, after several attempts to get me to talk to him, he gave up. He drove back home and sent me a text message asking me why I wouldn't speak to him. I responded by telling him he must want the police involved. He replied by letting me know that earlier I told him not to call me, but that I never said anything about text messaging. He was too damn smart for his own good. I let him know, that in due time, I'll speak to him, but not until I was ready.

# Chapter 18
# Friends or lovers

The football game was the least favorite highlight of the night at Maliq's house. The dinner was great and everyone was either slamming bones or playing cards. After a while, a few people at a time had begun to leave, including my sister and D. Dominic had to get some work done in the studio and he also had to get up early to go to his nine to five. But then, so did Aaries and I.

"You all are leaving so soon," Maliq asked them.

"Yeah man, I got to get some writing done and finish a track I've been working on," Dominic told them as they slapped palms.

"Alright then, keep it light."

"Well then, I guess that's my cue, as well, since I rode with them," I told Maliq.

"Oh, well if you want to stay, I'll take you back home. You know that. It's no biggy to me, whatever you want to do."

"Yeah Rain, just let Maliq take you home. Go on and stay and enjoy the rest of the night," Aaries said with an undertone in her voice that only I could detect.

"Ok."

After a while everyone else left and I helped Maliq clean up his kitchen. We also finished off an open bottle of wine and we started talking about everything under the sun - our past relationships, his son, our future goals, you name it. I was wiping down the counter tops when Maliq walked away to get an old photo album. We were clowning and reminiscing. There was an old picture where he had one of those gumby hair cuts and there was a picture of me when I had the poetic-justice-gucci-braids. We laughed so hard that I fell into his chest. I took a small step back. It was a slightly uncomfortable moment. All of a sudden, Maliq switched gears.

"You know Rain, I don't know if I told you or not, but you looked beautiful last night."

I had a nervous smile on my face. "Thanks."

When Maliq moved closer to me, I started breathing heavier and my heart was beating so fast that I thought for sure he could hear it through my chest.

"And your hair is beautiful, too. I like it straight like this," he said as he began to stroke the sides of my hair.

"And it wasn't just last night; I think you're beautiful everyday."

Maliq grabbed my chin and we looked into each other's eyes in a way that we had never experienced. He began to nuzzle on my lips until we were in a deep passionate kiss. And although it was probably only a few seconds, I could have stayed with him like this for an eternity.

I backed off. "Umm, I think I better go home now." I really didn't want to go home, but the way he was making me feel, I knew I'd be in trouble if I didn't go. And I didn't want to ruin our friendship.

"You're right. Let me get my keys." I knew he wasn't just going to get his car keys, because he went to the bathroom first. I've been with enough men to know what that was all about.

It was an uncomfortable ride home. Besides the music from the radio, that was it. We were dead silent. Neither one of us was about to bring up what just happened.

Once we were parked in front of my place, Maliq had to tell me something before I went inside.

"Rain, I'm sorry if I crossed the line, I just thought you…"

I cut him off mid-sentence. I did feel him at that moment, the same way he was feeling me, but I wanted to leave it at just that and not put too much thought into it otherwise we'd be more uncomfortable than what we already were.

"It's ok Maliq. It's ok. Goodnight."

# Chapter 19
# The Ex

The next morning when I got up all I could think about was Maliq and that kiss. It brought a smile to my face. I wondered if he was thinking about me in the same way. Not that it really mattered. I "A 1`mean after all, it wasn't like I was trying to be in a relationship with Maliq. We're best friends who got carried away after too many glasses of wine. Yeah, that's it. And I'm sure he feels the same. Enough of this, it's time for me to head into the restaurant.

We didn't open our restaurant for lunch until eleven-thirty in the morning, but I liked to arrive at least an hour to an hour and a half before to make sure everything is as it is supposed to be. Also, even though I mostly greet, I do all the ordering and I manage the staff as well.

When I got in everybody was in place and it looked like we were going to have yet another profitable day. The bartender was setting out the liquor. The servers were making sure their sections were looking good with proper place settings. And the chefs were ready to get things popping. *That's what I'm talkin' about, that's what I like to see.*

When I got into the back office, Aaries was entering numbers into the computer.
"Morning twin," I said as I plopped down on one of the rolling chairs. Aaries held her index finger up, telling me to hold on a second. She hates to be distracted while she is number crunching. She turned into a different person when she was all into that. After she saved her information, she turned and faced me.
"Hey sis, what's up," Aaries said with a smile on her face.
"You got it," I told her. We were always complimenting each other.
"You look like you're glowing. What's up with you?"
"Nothing," I said, slightly frowning, trying to hide my smile.
"Um-hmm, whatever Rain. Do I have to keep telling you, that I know you better than you know yourself?"
I brushed her off with the wave of my hand as I looked at some paper work with items I needed to order for the restaurant. Aaries got up from her chair and took two steps back as if to study me.

"Wait a minute," she said. "You got your little happy glow going on, a smile that you obviously can't get rid of, and look at that dress you got on.

You hardly ever wear a dress to work, you usually wear pants or a suit."
I simply shrugged my shoulders. Aaries squinted her eyes at me and looked at me suspiciously.
"So what did you and Maliq do last night after D and I left?"
I couldn't seem to bring my eyes up from the paper I was pretending to read, to even look at her.
"Not much, I helped him clean up and then we just watched a movie."
Aaries started smiling, she thought she had me.
"Oh really? What'd you watch?"
She caught me off guard and I started fumbling and mumbling my words. And my body language gave me away.
"Ooh! I knew it! I told you, y'all should hook up. So you and Maliq were bumping and grinding?"
"Ssh!" I jumped up and closed the office door. I didn't want anyone of the staff to overhear us.
"Get your mind out of the gutter Aaries. We didn't have sex."
"Well something happened, so spill the beans girl."
She sat back down and positioned herself in the chair like she was about to hear the juiciest gossip.
"We just..." I paused between words. "Accidentally kissed."

Aaries almost fell out of her chair laughing.
"How do you accidentally kiss somebody?"
I told her how everything happened so quickly. And how we were just talking and drinking and it just sort of happened. And I didn't mind sharing things with Aaries, but at first I didn't really want to tell her, because she can be so drastic at times. You give her an inch and she takes a mile. She will blow this little incident out of proportion.
We were laughing and choppin' it up so long, it was time to let our customers in.

By one o'clock, it was a pretty good lunch crowd. As I went from table to table to greet people and see how they were enjoying their meals, I saw a familiar face.
"Hi Rain."
"Hi," I said back to the familiar woman. It was Reah, Dominic's ex-girlfriend, before he married my sister. And she was sitting with a child. I didn't really care for her and she knew it. She tried to break them up when they were engaged. But I'm a woman about everything that I do and I played it off pretty good. I greeted her just like I do everyone else and I asked her how she was enjoying her food. She played along and tried to engage me in conversation. Clearly, I was not interested. She wouldn't let up.
"So how's Aaries," she asked.
"My sister is fine, Reah."

She nodded her head. "Oh where are my manners. I'm sorry Rain. This is my daughter, *Dominique*."
She would stop at nothing. She couldn't have Dominic so she went and got herself pregnant and named her child after him. Pathetic! Some typical shit a woman with ghetto mentality would do. Once again, I kept my composure and I smiled.
"Nice to meet you Dominique." She didn't say much except thank you, and she smiled.
Before I could dismiss myself, Aaries walked up to Reah's table just as she was reaching for her purse to leave.
"Leaving so soon, Reah," she said with a smirk on her face.
"Hey Aaries, what's up girl?" Reah was so fake it was pitiful. "Long time no see, but it's time for us to go anyway. I have to take her to see her father. We all have an appointment."
Aaries frowned after Reah had walked off.
"What the hell did that trick want?"
"She and her daughter had just finished eating when I came out to greet." I didn't want to tell her the child's name; it would only make her mad.
"Yeah well, trust that anytime Reah is around, there is nothing but trouble. And I'm sure she's up to something."

## Chapter 20
## Jack's back

After Aaries had done her bookkeeping, I continued to handle other business. I was starting to get a little tired, so I decided to head home a little early. I trusted Wil, one of the bartenders who had keys, to lock up. As I was heading to my car, I saw Jack walking in my direction. He had his hands behind his back. I really didn't appreciate him coming to my place of business especially after I told him to let me contact him. He was awfully presumptuous. He must've known that I was about to say something, because he immediately wanted to give me an explanation. And just in case some shit was about to go down, I decided not to continue that walk to my car. When I saw him, I stopped in my tracks right outside the front of the restaurant. Several customers, as well as my staff, could see me.

"Before you get upset, I just wanted to say I didn't come to bother you. I simply wanted you to have these and to apologize for what I said to you the other night. You didn't deserve that."

He handed me what was behind his back - a bouquet of beautiful roses with mini-snickers buried in them. I gave a faint smile, not really wanting to give in. I was more impressed with the chocolate than I was the flowers. But nonetheless, they were pretty and they smelled good.

"They're nice," I said hesitantly. "And for the record, my favorite candy bar is a Take-5, but these little snickers will do," I told him, trying to give him a hard time.

"So noted, Rain. Hey listen, I was wondering if you want to come to my place for dinner tonight? Let me cook for you."

"See, you think you're slick. I thought you said all you came by to do was to drop these off."

He held up his hands as if to give up. "You're right Rain, I'm sorry. Anyway, I hope you enjoy them," Jack said as he turned to head back toward his car.

He looked like a wounded puppy with his tail stuck between his legs, walking away. I was so caught up in myself that I didn't realize how good he looked. He had on one of those three-piece suits that I like. Maybe I should meet him for dinner. At least, I wouldn't have to cook. After all, he did apologize and he tried to appease me with his little peace offering. It's the thought that counts.

"Jack wait."

He was halfway to his car when I crossed the street to catch up with him in the parking lot.

"What time is dinner?"
Jack was elated.
"Whatever time you want is good with me. Do you like Italian food?
"Love it."
"Alright, well just call me when you're headed out and I'll give you directions."
"Ok, I'll see you later on Jack."

# Chapter 21
# Busted

When Aaries arrived home, she checked her messages and saw that Dominic had called. He said he would be at the studio after work and he would see her later. She thought that it was strange that he called the home phone and not he cell phone; especially when he knew she probably wouldn't be home.

After she took a relaxing bath, she went downstairs to cuddle up on the couch and pulled out her book of *Sudoku*. She couldn't resist playing with numbers, even if it was a puzzle. About twenty minutes into it, she was halfway finished with a difficult one, when her phone rang. She frowned, because her concentration was being broken; but she thought it might be Dominic. She looked at the caller id on the phone and it simply said Fulton County.

"Hello?"
"Yes, is this Mrs. Giles?"
"Yes it is. Who's calling?"
"Yes, Mrs. Giles, this is Ronald Stevens calling from A1-DNA, in reference to the paternity testing

you and your husband had done on your daughter."
Aaries was confused. "I'm sorry, you have the wrong number. "
"Oh, I apologize. Perhaps, I did reach the wrong Giles' residence. Let me just verify. Aren't you married to Dominic Giles?"
"Yes."
"Oh good, then I did not misdial. I have the DNA results back from you, Mrs. Reah Giles, along with Dominic's DNA on a Dominique."
Aaries' heart sank. She felt like a brick had just been dropped into her stomach. But as hard as it was, she played along and pretended to be Reah.
"Oh yes, I'm sorry. How could I forget? Anyway, what was the outcome?"
"Yes ma'am it shows that Dominic Giles is a 99.99% probability of being the father of Dominique."
"Great," she said underneath tears. "Thank you for calling," she said hanging up the phone. It turns out that Reah purposely gave the DNA company Dominic's home phone number, and told them to specifically call at a time when she knew Dominic would not be home. This was precisely the reaction Reah wanted.

Aaries had so many emotions going at the same time. She didn't know what to feel or think. On one hand she was hurt, because she realized the man that she loves has been lying to her. On the other hand, she's angry and she wanted to hurt somebody. But she would at least give Dominic his time to come clean. She wouldn't assume anything. This could've been a trick, especially where Reah was concerned. That woman had been after her husband for years. Aaries told herself that D was different and she would handle things with him differently, especially since they were married. She wasn't going to treat him the same way she treated the other men before she got married. She was so emotional she couldn't finish her puzzle. What she did do was wait for Dominic to come home.

As soon as Dominic walked in, he dropped his bags by the door and went to kiss his wife. Aaries' attitude was dry and non-receptive.

"Hey Babe."

"Hey," she said dryly. "So did you get much done at the studio tonight?"

Dominic immediately looked down. "Yeah, we got a lot done," he said pretending to look for something in his bag.

He was nervous and Aaries knew it. She knew when her husband was lying.

"That's good. So did you work on any new songs?"

Dominic simply nodded.

"Really? What's the name of it and how does it go?
"Well right now, it's untitled."
"Sing a little of it for me."
"You know what Babe, my voice is just tired, that's all. I'll sing it another time for you though."
Now she knew for sure, he was lying. Dominic always loved to sing, especially if she asked him to sing for her. Besides he was a little too fidgety. He was nervous. Aaries knew she had him and decided to let the spider continue to weave his tangled web of deceit. Now she was simply toying with him.

"You know I had a great day at the restaurant today and guess who I saw?"
For a second Dominic seemed to breathe a little easier when he thought she had changed the subject and that he was off the hook.
"Who Babe?'
"Reah."
"Reah?"
"Yeah, you know your ex-girlfriend Reah. She's back in Atlanta. Did you know that?"
He could barely look her in the eyes. "No. What was she doing there?"
"Well, why else would she have been there? To eat, of course. And she had the prettiest little girl with her. She said she was going to an

appointment and she was meeting her daughter's father there."
Dominic tried his best to sway to conversation elsewhere.
"That's interesting babe, but I don't want to talk about her. I just want it to be about you and I tonight."
"Hmm, that's interesting too D, 'cause I know if I had a daughter as pretty as *Dominique,* I would definitely want to talk about her."
He knew he was cold busted and there was nothing he could do now, except tell the truth.
"I just found out, I'm sorry," he said as he tried to reach out to touch Aaries' arm.
"Don't touch me!" she said as she stood up adjusting her bathrobe.
"I gave you enough chances to tell me the truth Dominic, but you just kept lying. It seemed like it was easy for you."
"Aaries, I swear it wasn't."
"I can't tell. You did it." Dominic couldn't say a word. They just sat there in silence staring at one another.
"So tell me how long have you've known that Reah was back in town? And when the hell were you going to tell me that you had a child?"

He tried to explain to her that he meant well, and that he didn't want to tell her until he knew for sure.

"So you knew about this since before the holidays and you didn't trust me enough to let me know as soon as you knew?"
"I did what I thought was best. And during the holidays, I only thought that there was a possibility that I may have a child with Reah."
"Well your best is unacceptable, D. So have you been spending time with them?"
"I've been spending time with my daughter," he said correcting her.
"Whatever D! You've been spending time with *them* all this time, but you just found out what the results were. So all this "studio time" you've been talking about was a lie, right?"
Dominic felt so bad. But he didn't want to make it any worse than what it was. He fessed up. He nodded.
"Well I'll tell you what, since you been sneaking around to spend time with your *other* family, then why don't you go be with them."
"Aaries you're talking crazy."
Something came over Aaries and she just could not take the lies. She began to yell at him.
"No! You are a liar! I remember a few months ago when you said if we don't have trust, then we don't have anything and you were right. I don't trust you, so we don't have anything Dominic. Not now. And you know what really hurts me is that when I married you, not only was I in love

with you, but I wanted to marry you because you were different than the other men I had been with. I guess I was wrong; you are just like all the rest. So you go on and pack your bags and go be with your child. You always wanted a family, so I guess now you have one."

"Look Aaries, this is my house too and…"

She cut him off mid-sentence. He thought he was going to regain his courage by laying down the law to Aaries. Not!

"Get your shit and get out!" she yelled at him.

Dominic decided not to push her and just honored her wishes. He went upstairs to get some clothes and other items. He knew Reah would be more than happy to accommodate him, but he knew better. He called his friend Barren and asked if he could crash there for a few days.

Before he walked out, he looked at his wife. He could tell that she had been crying.

"So what does this mean for us Aaries?"

"It means I don't want to talk to you right now. Goodbye!" she said pointing at the door.

"I'll leave, but first tell me how you found out."

"It doesn't matter how I found out. I just did. Now get out!"

Dominic walked out and they were both hurt. There were so many more questions Aaries wanted to ask him, but she couldn't take anymore. She just wanted to be alone.

# Chapter 22
# Feeling woozy

Before I headed out to Jack's house, I checked myself out in the mirror from head to toe. I put my hair up in a bushy ponytail, sported a gray, off-the-shoulders sweater, a pair of jeans with a belt that hung off of the hips, and some gray ankle boots. The eighties were making a strong come back.

As I dashed out the house, I looked down at Aaries' house and I noticed only her car was present. I guess Dominic must've been at the studio or something. While I sat in the car, waiting for it to warm up, I threw a little color on my lips. Then I called Jack to get the directions to his house. I put him on speakerphone and wrote the directions down on a piece of paper I had in my purse. He gave me the directions and told me he lived off of Sugarloaf Parkway. Apparently, he had more money than I anticipated, because his next-door neighbor is Michael Vick. And those homes were far from cheap. And before I got to his house, I ducked into a grocery store about one exit away from Jack's place. I wanted to surprise him with something.

Once I arrived, Jack greeted me at the door and gave me a kiss on the cheek. He was slowly but surely trying to make his way back into my good graces. Right about now, he was still a little unsure of himself. He looked good; he had on a black pullover sweater and some slacks. Different from the normal suit and tie he usually wears, but still nice. "Well come on in," he said. "Let me show you around."

"Wait one second," I told him with a smile on my face. I ran back to my car to get something and held it behind my back until I approached the door. "What's behind your back," he asked inquisitively. I presented to him, a miniature cake that you can get from any supermarket…it read…Happy Birthday! "I know I'm late with the cake but I had no idea that it was your birthday when we went to New Orleans. You should've told me sooner. Well, anyway, Happy Birthday Jack," I said to him giving him a kiss on the cheek. Jack stood there in awe. He seemed as if he were getting ready to cry. "This is very thoughtful and so nice. You have no idea what this means to me." And since the whole thing seemed kind of awkward I decided to break what seemed like tension in the room. "Well alright, put that cake in the fridge and take me on a tour of this grand mansion that you call a house.

When I walked in I have to admit, I was impressed with his pad. It was more than a house; it was a mansion. He had an east and west wing with a hallway that divided the two sides of the house and an elevator going between three stories. And when he took me on a "tour", I must have counted at least five or six bedrooms on each side of the house. There was also a large aquarium in the living room and a pool table with red felt, down in the basement, which he made into a game room. He said he thought of the design himself and had it built from the ground up.

Jack told me he was almost finished preparing our meal. He told me to watch TV and relax in the living room. All of a sudden, something seemed wrong. I felt like Aaries was in trouble or something serious was going on. I felt somewhat lightheaded and almost sick to my stomach. As twins, we never felt each other's pain or anything like that, but rather had some sort of an ESP thing going on. I immediately pulled out my phone and called her at home.

When she picked up, she sounded depressed.

"Aaries what's wrong? Are you ok?"

"I'm alright", she told me unconvincingly.

"Look, you know how I get when I think something is wrong. Now I'm feeling sick, so

don't play with me Aaries. What's going on with you?"
It wasn't that Aaries was ashamed or anything like that. In fact, she always opened up to me. But Aaries just wanted time to think at the moment. She just wanted some time alone. But she managed to vaguely tell me why Reah was in town and that the DNA folks had called her and she told Dominic to hit the road.
I told her I was on the other side of town and that I would be there shortly. She needed me.
"No, Rain. Right now, I just want to clear my head. But we can talk in the morning, when I'm fresh. What are you doing all the way over near Sugarloaf?"
"I'm having dinner with Jack."
She didn't have the energy to argue with me, so she let that one slide.
"Alright, well you enjoy your evening with Jack and we'll talk tomorrow."
"Are you sure? I mean are you going to be ok Aaries?"
"Yeah, just bring me a plate," she said jokingly.

After she and I hung up, I still had a good mind to cut this date short and go and check on my sister. But at the same time, I wanted to respect her wishes and give her some breathing space. After all, I would see her in the morning.

Ten minutes later the smell of garlic and other spices permeated through Jack's house, and it was making me hungry. Once everything was prepared, Jack placed everything beautifully on the table. He called me to the dining room and we enjoyed our salads first. The main course was cannelloni stuffed with ricotta cheese, chicken and broccoli topped with parmesan cheese, and a white sauce. He also made shrimp and lobster fettuccine. Everything was divine, but way too much food for two people. And I got stuffed way too quickly. That was because I was eating the breadsticks along with sipping on some red wine.

After dinner, Jack asked me if I wanted to watch a movie. Instead of a movie, we decided upon some comedy. I sure could use a laugh right about now. We chose the first season of the *Chappelle Show.* Before Jack put it on, he asked me if I wanted some more wine. I obliged him.

When he came back out of the kitchen, we sat a little close to each other. I let my guard down enough for him to put his arm around me. About twenty minutes into the show, I started to drift off. I guess I was more tired than I realized. Or maybe I just didn't realize that Jack had dropped a sleeping pill into my wine. He was smart enough to only put one in my drink. He wanted to make sure that I woke up feeling refreshed or like I just drifted off into a nap, rather than feeling tired and groggy, the way victims of Rohypnol or users of Valium feel. He didn't want me to feel as though a sledgehammer had been dropped on me. Nor did he want me to suspect he put something in my drink. Unbeknownst to me, Jack had some serious plans. That night he sure was busy. While I was sleeping, he went through my purse and got my house key. He made a spare at Wal-Mart. He also intercepted a text message that I had received from Maliq. Maliq sent a text message about the date and time of his court hearing. Jack started to send a bogus reply back, but he thought it would raise suspicion, so instead he simply deleted it, but not before he jotted down Maliq's phone number. He planned on googling him too, with the same reverse search he used on me.

When I awoke a few hours later, I was in Jack's bed fully clothed and I still had my boots on, with a blanket draped over me. I got out of the bed and followed the noise downstairs to the living room where Jack was watching TV.

"Hey sleepy head?"

"What happened Jack?"

"Nothing happened except that you fell asleep on me, that's all. I put you in my room so I wouldn't disturb you. But don't worry, you can sleep in there and I'll sleep in one of my other rooms. I have plenty."

"Oh, well I think I should leave now."
"Leave? Rain it's after one in the morning, and that's a long drive from here over to the south side of the city. Why don't you just stay until a reasonable hour and then drive back? It's no big deal. Like I said I have plenty of space and I won't bother you, because I'll use the other room."

I looked at him suspiciously, but then I agreed to stay.

He showed me where the fresh linens were and he gave me a t-shirt to sleep in.

# Chapter 23
# Inspector Gadget

A few hours later, Jack got up to cook me some breakfast, but I was only interested in hitting the highway. I wanted to check on Aaries.

Meanwhile, Jack took the opportunity to stay home and handle some business of his own. The internet was literally the world at your fingertips. You could find anything. And that's what Jack intended on doing. He used one of those people search websites and did a reverse search on Maliq. It took him a while, but he found what he was looking for. He typed in the address and realized that Maliq lived near Six-flags.

Jack's mind was racing one thousand miles a minute. He wanted me in a bad way. And he felt like if he couldn't have me, no one would. He planned to get rid of Maliq sooner rather than later. And there was no telling what he planned on doing with the key he duplicated.

As he thought of me, he smiled. He reached up under the couch and grabbed his photo album. Jack had been busy. Apparently, during the few days I didn't speak to him, he was following me and took pictures of me whenever he had the opportunity. A lot of the pictures were taken right outside of my restaurant. His album seemed to be somewhat of a collage. One of the pictures showed me giving Maliq a friendly hug. This enraged Jack. He threw the photo album so hard across the coffee table that he broke a vase that was sitting just to the left. Jack really did allow his mind to get the best of him. And he had some serious plans for Maliq.

# Chapter 24
# Sisterly advice

I decided that since I had left Jack's place so early, that I would go home and get myself ready to go into the restaurant first. That would give Aaries a little time to get out of bed.

I walked over to her house and knocked on the door. I started to use my key, but I decided to let her answer the door. Just because we're sisters doesn't mean we have free reign over each other. Besides, I respect the fact that she's married now.

When Aaries opened the door her hair was pulled back and she was dressed in big baggy sweatpants and covered in perspiration.

"What's up Rain", she said still panting from her workout.

"You already know what's up. I came to check on you", I said as I walked into her living room.

"Well as you can see, I'm good," Aaries tried to speak so nonchalantly.

"Girl, whatever. You must think you're talking to one of the staff at the restaurant. This is me here. Now what's up? Start talking. You don't have to act like everything is cool with me."

"Once I said that, she let it all out."

"D has been lying to me. He's been chilling with that trick Reah and her daughter and the whole time telling me that he was going to the studio and laying tracks. What he was really doing was laying Reah."

"You really think he was sleeping with her?"

"I don't know. But it doesn't matter. He still lied about the whole thing. If he wasn't doing anything wrong, he wouldn't have been sneaking around. So I told him to get his shit and get the fuck out."

"Where is he staying?"

"I don't know and I don't care. He's probably with Reah."

"Well how did you find out? 'Cause I know he didn't come clean."

"Of course not, Rain. They won't ever incriminate themselves."

Aaries grabbed her towel and wiped her face and neck. She was still sweating from her workout on the elliptical machine. She gave her the run down on how she received a phone call from a man from the DNA company. As they were speaking, the phone rang. It was Dominic. Aaries looked at the caller id and rolled her eyes.

"Aaries, aren't you going to get that?"

"No. For what? It' just D, and I don't want to talk to him. I told him that. I'll talk to him when I'm ready and on my own terms, not his," she said as she walked into the kitchen to pour some coffee.

The phone finally stopped ringing. And just as we both sat down at the table to finish our conversation, the phone rang again that quickly. This was starting to infuriate Aaries.

"Rain, will you get that, 'cause he's not going to stop calling until he gets me. I know him."

"Ok."

"Hello? Yeah, hey D. Yes, of course she's here. No. She said she doesn't want to talk right now. What? Ok, I'll ask her."

I covered the phone and held it at my side. "Aaries, he says he's desperate and he wants to know if you will just at least listen to him. He wants me to put him on speaker phone, so he can say what he needs to say to you."

Aaries looked at me like I was crazy. "I don't even know why you even bothered with asking me that. The answer is still no."

"Dominic, she doesn't want anything to do with you right now. No. Ok, I'll tell her. Bye."

"He said to tell you that he loves you."

"Psssh!" She motioned her hand and made a sound as if to say whatever.

"Anyway, enough about me. What's up with you, Rain? What is up with you and Jack?"

I told her about my date with Jack last night and that we had a good time. I told her I enjoyed his company and that was that. No more, no less.
"Umm, well you know I don't really care for Jack, so what about Maliq? See, you need to quit playin' and go on and do what you really want to do with him. Both of you guys are playing with the idea right now."
All I could do is smile. My sister knows she has a way with words. She did make me wonder a little bit though. What if?

I cut our conversation short and told her I was going to work. She said she would be in late. She didn't plan on showing up until around three or so. I gave my sister a hug and told her I'd see her later.

## Chapter 25
## He makes me squirm

Once I arrived at the restaurant, I kept busy, especially since I was inundated with paper work and re-ordering products. Time flew by quickly and before I knew it, it was time for lunch. Just as I was about to leave my office to go and greet the customers, my phone rang.

"Lena's."

"Rain. Hi. It's Maliq." He was still a little uncomfortable with the way we left things. In fact, he was so unsure of himself, he felt the need to identify himself to me.

"Maliq, now you know I recognize your voice. We've only known each other for fifteen years. What's up?"

This changed our tones a little and put us both at ease. One thing about me is if I'm a little uncomfortable with something, I can always use a little comedy to smooth it over.

Maliq gave off a laugh of relief.

"I don't know why I did that; but anyway, what I'm calling for is important. I sent you a text the about the court date last night and you didn't respond." He quickly shifted gears and got

straight down to business when it came down to his son.
I told him that I didn't get a text message from him. That really didn't strike me as being odd, especially with a cell phone. Calls get dropped from time to time and sometimes information does not come through. Regardless, I took the information from Maliq and I told him I would definitely have his back. He was a good man and his son deserved to be with him and vice-versa.

Then the conversation started to take a turn of its own. Maliq started asking me questions about Jack and I.
"So, were you out with Jack last night?"
"Yes," I said wondering where this conversation was going.
"You two sure have been spending a lot of time together lately.
I mean do you really dig him like that?"

Normally I would not have felt funny answering these questions with Maliq, but his tone was different, almost like he was jealous or something.
"Maliq, what kind of question is that? Of course, I like him; otherwise, I wouldn't be spending time with him. Besides, why are you asking me these questions about Jack?"
"I don't know Rain. Like you said, we've known each other for years. I know what type of men are

good for you, and he ain't it," Maliq stated with authority. "It's just something that's not right about him."

I let out a hearty laugh. "I know you are not talking. What about that girl you used to mess with a few years ago? What was her name," I asked as I began snapping my fingers as if that were going to help me recall her name a lot quicker. "Um, I think it started with a 'J'. Jenny, or Jamie or something like that?"

"You mean Janai?"

"Yeah her. Now talk about someone who isn't right for you. The two of you were like night and day." The two of us just laughed.

"I know Rain. I'm just saying I think you can do better."

I decided to humor him.

"Better how?"

"I don't know, maybe getting with someone who knows how to take care of you and really knows and understands you."

"Any suggestions," I said to him playfully.

Before we were able to finish our conversation, one of my chefs came to inform me that the inspector had arrived to check out the restaurant.

*Maliq and I?* Nah!

# Chapter 26
# Order in the court

About two weeks had passed. Jack and I had been spending quite a bit of time together. It almost seemed as if we had been seeing each other every other day. Tonight was one of those nights. I decided I just wanted to spend a nice quiet evening at home. Jack and I ordered a pizza and got some DVD's to watch.

We were all comfy and cozy on my couch when the phone rang shortly after midnight. It was Maliq calling to remind me of the hearing tomorrow.

"Hey Maliq. Yep, I'm ready. I won't be late. In fact, I'll be there around seven-thirty in the morning, just to make sure I beat the morning traffic."

Jack readjusted his body from our cozy position once he heard Maliq's name. He decided that he wouldn't say anything this time. He didn't want to fall out with me like he did before.

Once I hung up with Maliq, I told Jack that I should probably get to bed since I had to be up so early. I decided to shower before going to sleep. Jack on the other hand must have been really tired, because he just jumped right in.

Although, we never had sex with each other before, we had slept in the same bed. I set my digital alarm clock for 6am and hopped in the shower.

Jack pretended to be sleep - only for a second, though. Once he realized I was actually in the shower, he reached over to my side of the bed and changed the settings on my alarm clock. He changed it, so that it went off at 6pm not 6am. Then he rushed up out of bed and went outside to slowly let the air out of my two back tires. At first, he thought he'd just do one tire. He changed his mind, because most people have at least one spare tire, but not two. He did this just in case I was to wake up before my clock went off. That way, I would be slowed down because I would have two flats.

Jack was getting back in the bed just as I was turning off the water.

The next morning when I awoke, I immediately panicked. It was daylight, which meant it had to be at least after seven o'clock in the morning. When I looked at the clock, I was exactly right. It was exactly 7:04am. That was definitely bad news, because it takes me at least forty minutes to get to the Fulton County courts and I hadn't even started getting ready yet. When I jumped up out of bed, I startled Jack.

"What's wrong?"
"I'm late," I told him as I looked at the alarm clock. I checked to see why the clock didn't go off.
"Damn," I said as I put my face in my hands. "I had it set for pm instead of am. I immediately started to run around. As I was brushing my teeth, I ran to my closet to see what I could wear that didn't require ironing. Luckily I found a beige suit that was still draped in plastic from the dry cleaners. After I rinsed, I quickly pulled on some pantyhose and put my suit on. I had no time for vanity, so I simply pulled my hair back in a ponytail to save time. I knew I would never make it by seven thirty, but at least I could try and make it by eight o'clock. And hopefully, they wouldn't need my testimony right away. As I was doing all this, Jack was in the other room putting on the clothes he wore from last night and smiling at his little charade.

By the time I finished getting ready, it was7:37am. Jack and I each got into our perspective vehicles. Jack gave me a rushed kiss on the cheek and sped off. Or at least he pretended to. What he really did was drove around the corner where I could not see him and waited for me to pull out. When I pulled out it felt like I was running over two boulders. I got out the car and became frantic when I saw both rear tires were flat. I was so upset, I almost started to cry. Normally, I'm cool as a cucumber and have it all together, but today I was a mess. The thing that bothered me the most is that Maliq was counting on me. I told him I would be there for him. I don't want the judge to deny him his son just because I couldn't get there.

I had AAA, but court would be over by the time they'd arrive. I picked up my cell phone to give Jack a call to come and take me; I noticed I missed a call. It was Maliq and he hadn't bothered to leave a message. I didn't call him, because I didn't want to worry him. Instead I called Jack to come back to get me.

"Jack, I have two flat tires. Can you come back to get me? It's important, because I have to be at Fulton County for court."

"I'm already on the freeway Rain. Besides, traffic is horrendous," he said lying through his teeth.

I told Jack never-mind. I don't know why I didn't think of it before, but I went down the street to Aaries' house and I told her I needed her car and that I'd be back in a few hours or so.

Traffic was so ridiculous on any given morning in Atlanta, especially if there is an accident. And that's exactly what happened today. A fender-bender…Why today? I tried reaching Maliq by cell, a few times, but his phone was off. Cell phones were not allowed to be on during court proceedings.

By the time I got to the courthouse, it was close to nine-thirty. When I arrived inside and had my purse checked for weapons, the officers told me what floor to go on. When I arrived, I inquired with a bailiff coming out of one of the rooms, where Maliq's room would've been. He informed me that all of the rooms were in alphabetical order as to the last name of the plaintiff. In that case, the R's would be somewhere close to the end of the hall. All of the rooms had the name and the case type on the outside of the door.

When I walked in I saw a bailiff and a few spectators. It always struck me as strange that people would want to go and listen to court cases on people they didn't know anything about.

I started to really worry when I didn't see Maliq. Hell, I didn't even see Tasha, his ex-wife. This was not a good sign. I decided to at least call him again and find out what was going on. But what I feared was true.

"Yeah," Maliq answered the phone in a low irritated voice.

"Maliq, it's me. I'm at the courthouse, but I don't see you."

"Well, take a wild guess Rain. Court is over. Thanks for showing up *friend*."

"Maliq, I'm so sorry. I meant to be there for you. Everything just went wrong today. First, my clock didn't go off. I had it set for pm rather than am and then I called Jack to come back to the house to pick me up, but…"

"Jack?" he cut her off mid-sentence. "What, he spent the night or something?"

"Yes, but it's not what you think Maliq, I just…"

"Oh, so it's like that now? I get it, you're just getting all caught up with dude and now you're neglecting your friends and responsibilities."

"No, I told you it's not what you think."

"Oh, you don't have to explain anything to me. It's cool if that's how you're rollin' now. What's not cool is giving me your word and breaking it. Like you said, we've known each other since junior high and you know I don't ask for anything, but if I do, it must be for something real important. You should know that Jaden is the most important thing in my life…my son, Rain. So for you to not be able to come through for me in my time of need is unacceptable Rain. I trusted you and you let me down."

All I could do is cry as I sat and listened to Maliq vent. I knew I wasn't being irresponsible, but right now I realized he just needed to vent, so I didn't say too much.

"Maliq, you know I have never let you down until now. I know it won't change anything, but all I can do is apologize. I don't appreciate you insinuating that all this happened, because I'm involved with Jack."

"Well, you don't have to worry about it anymore."

Maliq hung up on me. I couldn't believe it. Anyone else under normal circumstances, I would've called back just to cuss them out. But this was different. I had to handle this delicately.

## Chapter 27
## Love never left

Shortly after I returned Aaries' car, I was in the middle of telling her what happened with Maliq, and Dominic walks through the door. At first I didn't know what to think. Maybe they had got back together and she hadn't told me yet. But that was not the case.

Aaries looked at him up and down. "What the hell are you doing here Dominic?"

"I'm moving back in," he said as he laid his bag on the couch.

"What? No, you're not. I told you to get out and that you couldn't come back until I said so."

"Look Aaries, I'm tired of this. I've tried to get you to talk to me, but you won't. So now I'm back. This is my house too and we're gonna sit down and talk about this shit once and for all."

I thought now would be a good time for me to leave. I gave Aaries a kiss on the cheek and told her I'd see her later.

She walked out of the kitchen to the living room toward Dominic. She had her arms crossed and really wasn't trying to hear what he had to say.

By this time Dominic was sitting on the couch and he moved his bag to the floor.
"So what's so important that you had to barge your way back into this house D?"
"Us, of course. I mean I can't even believe you're asking me that. All I think about is you. I can't even concentrate when I go into the studio. I miss you. Don't you miss me?"
Aaries was still standing up near the couch looking down at Dominic. "Look D, it's irrelevant how I feel. But all I know is that you lied. So just say what the hell you want to say and then get out. I'm serious about that," she said with her arms crossed.

"Look Aaries, I'm not playing games. I told you, I'm moving back in. We're gonna talk about this shit and iron it out and that's that. So you can either forgive me and make things smoother or you can continue to be mad at me indefinitely; and we'll just be up in here like we're roommates. But I'm not leaving. And will you sit down while I'm talking to you?"

Aaries humored him but she still had her arms crossed. Other than cussing him out, she felt like this was her only form of defense.
"Look Aaries, I know I messed up. I lied to you. I kept the information from you, because I didn't want you to be upset. I should've trusted you more and let you know everything from the

beginning. And believe me, I planned on telling you once I knew everything to be true. This way, if it wasn't true, then things would go on as normal for us."

Suddenly Aaries just became emotional. "Well let me tell you how I feel. I'm angry, I'm hurt and I'm sad all in one. When I got that phone call from the DNA lab, I was so hurt Dominic. And it really didn't have much to do with the fact that I thought you could be cheating on me. It had more to do with the fact that you didn't trust me enough with the information; and that this bitch got one up on me. She knows some information about *my* husband that I don't even know, whether it's true or not."

It felt like a weight had been lifted off of her shoulders. She felt somewhat liberated having gotten that up off her chest. It didn't necessarily mean that she would forgive him, but she felt empowered again by releasing all that pent up stress.

"I know Aaries and I'm sorry. I made a huge mistake. I can't change the past. I can't take that stuff back, but all I can do is promise you that nothing like this will ever happen again. I mean it," he said as he moved in closer to her stroking her chin. This softened her a little, but not enough for her to completely forgive Dominic.

He wanted to know more about the phone call and what it entailed. This was the first he'd known about any phone call. After they put two and two together, Dominic was able to figure out that Reah set this whole thing up. Although he and Aaries purchased a new house together just before they were married, he still kept the same home phone number. Reah was very aware of this. There were several times she called from an unknown number just to hear Dominic's voice and hung up. Of course, she'd never be dumb enough to call about this DNA business, but she had someone else do it.

"You know what I think Babe," Aaries said to Dominic. "If she went that far to set up the phone call, she's clever enough to set the whole charade up. I mean Dominique may not even be your child. I wouldn't put it past her." By this time Aaries had mellowed out completely.

Dominic nodded his head. "I thought about that, too. Don't worry. We're going to get to the bottom of this. We're going to catch her in her lies, all in good time, but first I just want you to know how much I've missed you."

He leaned in and kissed her. She didn't resist, because she knew that she missed him too. It was the kind of kiss that got the dick hard and the pussy wet. They didn't have any choice but to get buck wild right there on the sofa. The two of them were so horny they didn't even bother to take off all of their clothes. Dominic just pulled his pants down to his ankles and Aaries was already dressed for work and she had on a skirt. She just lifted it up and sat on top of Dominic and rode him like she was in a western style rodeo.

As soon as they were done, Aaries called me to let me know that she wouldn't be in at all today. She decided to spend the day with her husband.

## Chapter 28
## Second thoughts

It had been a few weeks and I still had not heard from Maliq. I just knew by now, I would have heard from him. For the most part, I wanted to make sure I gave him his space. I figured he would eventually come around. I even tried to call him on two different occasions; but, just as I figured he would, he ignored me. That's it! This was the last straw; I had had enough.

I picked up my cordless phone and dialed Maliq at home. No answer. Hung up, then I dialed his cell, big surprise; still no answer. I decided this time to leave a message. And I let him have it.

"You know what Maliq…this is so ridiculous and immature of you. Now, I was nice enough to give you your space, but you're taking it too far. I can't believe that after all this time we've known each other, apparently you don't really know me at all. Do you really think that I would purposely miss something that was so important to you, especially where it concerns Jaden? You need to check yourself, Maliq. And to top it off, you never even gave me a chance to explain. You basically cussed me out and then hung up on me and I haven't heard from you since then. If you really want to throw a fifteen-year friendship down the drain, go right ahead."

When I hung up, my adrenalin was going about one hundred miles an hour. I was angry, but I was really more hurt than angry. After all, what I said was true. He should know that I wouldn't purposely do anything to hurt him or anyone in his family, especially where Jack, a man off the street is concerned.

And speaking of Jack, as fine as he is, I just don't think we're a match. We have things in common, but we're not really compatible. And there is a big difference. I think if people would recognize that early on in their relationships before marriage, there would be less divorces.

Over the last few weeks, we have spent a little more time together and there just didn't seem to be that spark. Not to mention, I really believe Jack thinks that I'm a pork chop, because he is smothering the hell out of me! He even planned some things that could've potentially been romantic, but I just wasn't feeling it with Jack. We went on a picnic. We went to the North Georgia Mountains, amusement parks, and all; but still nothing. Jack even took me on a shopping spree, but you can't buy someone's love or affection. And the last time we were together, it was quite obvious to me that we were in two different places, because he tried to hold my hand and I pulled away, because I wasn't feeling Jack like that. I on the other hand was making eyes with a man standing near us. I should've said something then, but I didn't. So the next time I see Jack, I'll just let him know. I'll let him down easy. I don't want to hurt his feelings, but I also want to be honest with him and myself.

# Chapter 29
# St. Valentines Day

If it weren't for the fact that Aaries called to remind me that she and Dominic were going on a weekend excursion, I wouldn't have known it was Valentine's Day.

It so happened to be on a Saturday and for once in my life, I decided to do absolutely nothing. No ripping and running, no errands, no shopping, nothing! It was just a typical day to me and I showered and lounged around in my sweat pants and a t-shirt and watched movies all day. It was just me, myself and I, or so I thought.

I was disturbed when I heard my doorbell ring. I decided to ignore it. After all, I wasn't expecting any company and I figured it was just somebody selling something. Then they rang it two more times, a little more urgently.

I walked to the front of the house and peeked out the peephole. *What the hell*, was all I thought when I saw Jack standing at my door. He's cool, but now I felt like he was overstepping his boundaries. Coming over unannounced and uninvited is a no-no. Usually women do this to men, but I guess turnabout is fair play.

I swung the door open and let into him without so much as a hello. "Jack, would you appreciate if I just popped up at your house?"

A stunned Jack just stood there for a moment and then answered with ease.

"Actually I wouldn't mind. You are welcome at my home any time," he said smiling.

"Well for the last time Jack, don't do it. It's an invasion of my privacy and it shows a lack of respect on your part, as well."

That knocked the smile right off of his face and it quickly faded into disappointment.

"I'm sorry Rain, I just wanted to surprise you with this," he said as he handed me a red present with pink trimming. "Happy Valentines Day."

I felt bad only for a second. After all, I did tell him not to show up unannounced. We stood in the doorway for a second before I allowed him to come in. I had decided to take this opportunity to call things off with him.

"Thanks," I said giving him a slight half-smile. "Come on in."

We walked past the kitchen and into the living room where we sat for a moment and had a heart to heart. I looked down at the beautifully wrapped present and handed it back to him. Even though I was curious as to what it could be, I didn't want to accept the gift and lead him on.

Finally, Jack was able to pick up on something. He became a little bit more serious.
"What's wrong," he asked.

I told him how I thought that he was a wonderful and attractive man, but we just weren't a match. I told him that he was going to make some woman happy, but that woman wasn't me. He suddenly became very angry.
"And just how much of this has to do with Maliq?"
"None of it has to do with Maliq. I can make my own decisions. You're just not the guy for me."
Then, just like that, his mood changed again. This time he seemed to become sad. "Was it something I said or did? Tell me what I can do to make it better?"
The begging had become very unattractive.
"Jack, it's nothing like that. It's just that we don't really have that chemistry. No connection."
Once again his mood changed to melancholy. "Well, go ahead and open your gift. I want you to have it anyway."

Before I could open it, my doorbell rang again. It was Maliq. I was surprised to see him. He had an apologetic look on his face and I had a look of disdain on mine.

"So what's up," I said.
"You."

"Oh really?"
"Yeah really. Look I came by to apologize. It was stupid of me to even think that you would purposely stand me up and I'm sorry."
"Alright, but do me a favor. I hate to even ask this, but can you come back by here a little later? I'm kind of in the middle of something with Jack."
"Oh I see," he said as if I was sticking it to him again.
"It's not like that Maliq, just come back by ok?"
"Yeah," he said walking back toward his car.

I wanted to tell him that I was ending things with Jack, but Jack was within ear range. Even though he couldn't see who was at my front door from my living room, I'm sure he could hear us.

I sat back down next to Jack on the couch and decided to at least open up the gift to see what it was, I was curious. After I unwrapped it, I think my chin actually hit the floor in amazement. He got me a three-piece set of jewelry - a platinum princess tiara necklace with teardrop cut diamonds, a matching bracelet and, a ring. Absolutely flawless!

"It's gorgeous Jack, but it's too much. I can't accept such an extravagant gift."

He said he wanted me to have it and that I deserved it. He wanted me to have it regardless of the fact that I had just served him his pink slip. I know I was just being greedy, but I accepted them. I tried them on and admired myself in the mirror on the adjacent wall across from the couch. I thanked Jack and told him that I had someone coming over soon. He seemed disappointed again, but begrudgingly left my house. I was curious to find out what Maliq had to talk about.

## Chapter 30
## Surprise

That same evening, Maliq came back. He called to let me know that he was on his way. Since I was cleaning my kitchen, I told him to just let himself in when he got here. He did just that.

When he got here, I cut straight to the chase. "So what did you want to talk about," I asked him dryly.

"Look, I came by to apologize. It was stupid of me to even think that you would purposely stand me up and I'm sorry."

I was easy when it came to Maliq. After several years of friendship, it was very easy for me to forgive him.

I smiled. "Alright," I told him.

He smiled back; and then we both just busted out laughing. It was like we both wanted to be mad at each other, but we knew it wouldn't last. We knew each other far too well.

"As a peace offering, I got you something," Maliq said eagerly.

*Damn, two gifts in one day, I thought.* This ought to be good.

"Really? You didn't have to get me anything, Maliq."

"I know, but I wanted to. Now I want you to go in the living room and keep your eyes closed until I tell you to open them, ok?"
"Ok." This time I was grinning from ear to ear like a kid on Christmas morning. I heard Maliq go out and come back three times. The first two times, I heard him swing the door open and place something on the floor near the kitchen. The last time he closed the door behind him and came into the living room.

"Ok, open your eyes."
When I opened my eyes, I was so surprised. He handed me a black and white, shorthaired, furry little kitten. It was so cute and no bigger than one of my hands. He knew I had been talking about getting a cat for about a year now. He figured that I would never get one myself and he took it upon himself to get one for me. Not to mention that Maliq has given me a Valentine's Day gift every year since college, but there seemed to be something more to this.

Maliq began to smile and I continued to dote over the cute little kitten. It purred and meowed the whole time I was petting it. I finally decided to lift it up to assess the sex. It was a female. She was a cute kitten with green eyes. I put her down long enough for her to smell her way around the house and become familiar with it.

Maliq was standing in front of the window across from the couch and I ran up to him and gave him the biggest hug. He put his arms around me and that was all she wrote. He started pulling my sweater off as we kissed and I began to unbutton his shirt. The bottoms and the drawls fell off; and the next thing I knew, we were on the couch butt-booty-naked handling our business. I think we were both stunned as to what just happened. We just laid on the couch for a minute. Neither one of us said anything, but I know I was thinking, *what in the hell have I just done*. I just slept with my best friend. We crossed that line and we can never go back. I just happened to look down on the carpet and I saw the kitten staring up at us and she let out a faint meow. All we could do was laugh. I grabbed a throw blanket that I had lying on the couch. I covered myself and went to my bedroom to retrieve my bathrobe.

When I had come back, Maliq had gone to the bathroom. I noticed a few items on the kitchen floor on my way back to the living room. It was a whole kitty starter kit. There was a small bag of dry cat food, feeding bowls, a litter box with a scoop, one container of litter, a blanket, and a cat bed.

He was just walking out when I saw all of this. "You got all of this for me?"

"Yeah. I mean it just didn't make sense for me to get you a cat without all the stuff that goes along with it. That's like buying a child a toy that requires batteries and giving him the toy without buying him some batteries."
"Thank you Maliq, you're so sweet."
That was what I loved about Maliq. He was sweet and thoughtful. He knew it was the little things that stood out with me, not the big extravagant gifts. Nothing wrong with them, but that's not what grabs my heart.
"You're welcome."
Maliq went on to say that he knew I had been talking about getting a cat for a while and he figured I'd never do it, so he got one for me.
"By the way Rain, this is also your valentines day gift, too. You know I haven't missed one since we were in college."

I thanked him and told him to help me think of a name. I fiddled around with a few: Casper, Panther, and Oreo. I hated when people gave their pets human names. But I thought Oreo was cute, because she reminded me of the cookie itself. A black, top coat and a white underside. Then I just came up with something totally different from all of that - Mink. It fit her perfectly.

# Chapter 31
# Lunatic

Jack was fuming when he left my house. He heard everything that Maliq and I discussed. And as usual he thought something was going on with Maliq and I. This time, he was right and he saw it. He had parked on one of the main streets with the driver's side facing my living room window. He got an eyeful through his binoculars when he saw Maliq and I over by that window. Although, he didn't see us in the act, he didn't need to. Jack was smart and could put two and two together. Little did I know, he had some plans for Maliq and I.

Once Maliq left, Jack decided to follow him. He followed him all the way to his house. He needed to be able to get to Maliq's car, but Maliq parked in his garage. *So much for that*, Jack thought.

Instead he went on with plan-b. He parked and boldly walked up to Maliq's door and pounded like he was the police. When Maliq opened it, he didn't quite know what to think.

"The first question would be - how in the hell did you know where I lived? And the second one would be - what the hell do you want?"

"Maliq, I thought you were smarter than that," Jack said taunting him. "The internet is a savvy tool and the cool thing is it's open to the public."

"Why would you possibly want to know where I lived?"

"Because I'm here to let you know that Rain is mine and you need to stay away from her."

Maliq chuckled. He felt sorry for Jack, because he knew he was delusional.

"Really? Did Rain tell you that or is this something that you imagined in the sick twisted brain of yours?"

This infuriated Jack, especially when he thought he was being insulted. This took him back to a place when he was a child and all the kids used to tease him and call him crazy.

"Listen! You just better do as I tell you or you'll regret it."

That was it! He had pissed Maliq off. Maliq didn't like threats. He grabbed Jack's collar and pulled Jack toward him.

"Let me tell you something right now. You get your crazy ass out of here before I *beat* that ass, you hear," he said releasing Jack's sweater with a push, causing Jack to stumble backwards.

That was one thing that Jack could not do, was fight. He decided to go back to his car, but not without words first.

"You're gonna be sorry. You'll see." He made sure that he was close enough to his car, so that he could pull off quickly if need be. I guess he wasn't *that* crazy.

## Chapter 32
## Reunited

Dominic and Aaries were enjoying their weekend in the Bay area. Not only was it Valentine's weekend, but they were trying to rekindle their marriage and reconnect with each other.

Their lavish hotel suite was large enough to fit three rooms in it, including a parlor. It was furnished with an oversized round bed with goose down linens, decorated in rose petals, courtesy of her wonderful husband. Chaise lounges were also inside the room and on the balcony. The hotel suite was also equipped with a kitchen and a marbled-floor bathroom, including a bidet.

The happy couple was enjoying the breathtaking view of San Francisco on the balcony as they fed other fresh fruit in their bathrobes. Somehow the conversation turned, and they began discussing Reah.

"Do you really want to get into this now? It's our last night in the Bay. I mean after all, we are on a romantic getaway. I really don't feel like discussing your ex-girlfriend."

"I know Babe, but it's bugging me and I just want to get it out of the way and then we won't even have to talk about it any longer. Besides, it's a lot of stuff about this that just doesn't add up."

"If this trick was crazy enough to do all of that and set us up, the child might not even be yours Dominic."

Even though he knew there was some possibility, it actually bothered him to think that Dominique might not be his child. He had begun to spend a lot of valuable time with her.

"That's true Babe, but I doubt it," he said looking up into the clear blue sky.

"Ok, you doubt it, but you don't know for sure D. We owe it to our marriage to double check and see if Reah is lying or not. Hell, she did it once and she won't hesitate to do it again."

He nodded as he picked up a strawberry and dipped it in chocolate.

"Alright, I'll tell you what...as soon as we get back, I'll call Reah and tell her I want another test done."

"Thank you Baby," she said as she gave her husband a peck on the lips. "Just make sure it's a DNA company to our liking and not something that she has chosen. I don't trust that bitch."

## Chapter 33
## Jack-in-the-*hizouse*

Jack had begun to get a little psychotic. He was trippin' and trippin' hard! He just couldn't take my rejection. For the past three days, Jack started following me. Of course, I had no knowledge of this. But he was trying to figure out my routine and that's exactly what he accomplished. Two of those days, he followed me to and from work. After work, I would usually go somewhere before I went home. For a couple of those days, I went to the gym after work and then to the grocery store, usually to pick up some dinner. Regardless, Jack knew I never came straight home and that's exactly what he was hoping for.

On this particular day his replica of my house key came in handy. He also knew that Aaries lived down the street from me, so he was extra careful. He parked around the corner and walked the rest of the way to my house. He was even slick enough to come through the back door instead of the front door. Before he put the key in, he looked around to make sure no one was watching. When he felt comfortable, he put the key in. He had to pry it and shake it a few times before it would open. The door seemed to be stuck from lack of being opened, but he gave it one little extra nudge and voila! He was in and he wasn't at all startled by my burglar alarm. Jack had a few more tricks up his sleeve. During college, he had a part-time job at Alloy systems, coincidentally the same company that installed my home alarm system. This worked in his favor, because all Alloy systems had a default "dummy code". Technicians would use the dummy code to test alarm systems. It worked to cut it off, as well. All he had to do was find the alarm keypad. Since he had been to my house before and of course studied it from top to bottom, he knew exactly where to go.

Once he tricked the alarm, he went straight to my cordless phone and put a device near the battery. It was so small that it looked like it could be a part of the phone itself. Perfect! Now every time I answered my home phone, Jack would be able to hear every little sordid detail.

Before he left, he heard a loud hissing sound. It was Mink. She gave herself enough distance between herself and Jack to run if need be. Even though she was a kitten, she sensed bad vibes and didn't like it. Mink even lunged toward Jack sideways with her fur fluffed out and sticking up, in the same manner most cats do when they're in their aggressive fight or flight mode. This surprised Jack somewhat and he grabbed one of my throw pillows off of my couch and shooed Mink away.

"Go on, get out of here, you flea bitten varmint. Scram!"

Once Mink disappeared, he tossed the pillow back on the couch and vanished before anyone would notice him.

# Chapter 34
# Homie-lover-friend

I was so exhausted when I got home that I just dropped my gym bag on the floor and I plopped my body onto the sofa. I had had a long day. All I wanted to do was take a shower and relax in front of the TV.

Mink jumped up on the sofa and into my lap. I still wasn't used to the fact that I had a kitten. So of course, I indulged in spoiling her and I played with her for a few minutes.

When I finally mustered up the energy to get up and go shower, my phone rang. It was Maliq. We hadn't spoken in a few days or so. I wasn't even sure how I was supposed to be acting, even over the phone. When you sleep with your best friend, it changes things drastically. Was I supposed to continue to be his friend? Was I supposed to be his homey-lover-friend? Or was I supposed to be his girlfriend? Who knew? I sure didn't.

"Hey Maliq, what's up?"

"Hey yourself," he said somewhat seductively. "I think we need to talk. Do you mind if I come over there?"

It almost sounded like he was talking to me from a tunnel, because there was an echo as we spoke.
"No, that's fine. But give me a minute 'cause I was just about to jump in the shower. I'll leave the garage open for you."
"Alright, see you when I get there."

Once we hung up, all I could think about was his gorgeous body; and that I didn't know he had it like that in the bedroom. I see why his ex-wife acts a damn fool. She was whipped and I think I am, too. Gotta get me some more of that!

I stood up with Mink in one hand and scratched her under her neck. All she did was purr. When I was putting her down, I noticed something that struck me as odd. My throw pillows were on the same side. Usually, I have one on the left side of the couch and the other on the right. *Oh well*, I thought. I just chalked it up to an oversight.

After I took a shower, I put on a t-shirt and a pair of shorts. I had washed my hair as well, so I had a towel covering my head. No sooner than I sat back down was there a knock at my garage door. As I went to open it, Mink followed me. I let Maliq in, depressed the garage button; and we immediately walked to the couch.
"Did you want anything to drink?"
"Nah, I'm cool."

"Well I do, so hold on a second." I really didn't want anything to drink. I was frontin', because I was nervous. See you really gotta know what you're getting into before you sleep with your best friend. At least set some boundaries should be set. We just took a giant leap without thinking of the consequences.
"So what do you want to talk about Maliq," I asked him as I reached up for the cinnamon. I had poured myself a cup of chai tea.
"You and me," he said.
He startled me because his voice was closer than I anticipated. He had followed me to the kitchen. He pressed up against my backside and pulled the towel off of my head and kissed my neck. As I turned around, I thought it was about to be on and poppin' again. But instead he surprised me and took my hands into his and kissed one of them.

All of a sudden, he became very pensive. "I'm serious Rain. We need to talk about where we go from here. I mean we crossed a line that we can never reverse. Personally, I'm not trying to reverse it." He had a little smile on his face.
"Me neither. I'm glad it happened."
"Good so you don't regret it then, right?"
All I could do was shake my head and smile.
"I'm glad, 'cause I'm in love with you Rain and I have been for some time now. I mean what's not to love? We're great friends and have been for so

long. We have fun together and you make me laugh. You are always there for me, and Jaden too, for that matter. And you fine as I don't know what. I can't resist that. I had to have you. But more importantly, I want us to be together and I want to know if you want the same thing?"
I nodded. "Yes, Maliq. And I want you to know that I love you too," I said as I looked him in his eyes and tried to dig deep into his soul.
While we were still holding hands, he pulled me to him. As we kissed, my damp hair brushed up against the side of our faces. I was hot and ready to go, but Maliq slowed me down. He said we didn't need to rush. He took me by the hand once again and led me into my bedroom.
"The rest of the night belongs to you, Rain. I want you to know just exactly how I feel about you. All you need to do is relax and enjoy. I'll get mine another time."

At first I wasn't sure what he was talking about until he began to show me. He pulled off my t-shirt. He started kissing me on my neck and worked his way down to my breasts where he kissed and licked for about ten minutes. He also worked my shorts off and began sliding his finger up and down my clitoris. Damn, I could've come just like this. But I held back. I wanted to savor it and enjoy the ride. He pulled his shirt off and told me to straddle him. More specifically, he told me to sit on his face. That man was so talented with his tongue. He pleasured me so many different ways. I just couldn't resist. I think I lost count of how many times I "came" after about six. I think he just gave a new definition to the phrase "speaking in tongues".

# Chapter 35
# You go girl!

Dominic and Aaries were on their way to pick up Dominique to take another DNA test. Of course, Reah had no knowledge of this. And this time, Aaries was serious. She wanted to be there with Dominic every step of the way. She didn't trust Reah as far as she could throw her. But before they left the house, Aaries came by to check on me. We hadn't spoken since before she and D went on their excursion. She came by to give me the business and of course she didn't knock. She used her key and let herself in. When I heard the door open, I scrambled out of the bed for my bathrobe. Maliq immediately covered his bottom half with the bedspread. I closed the door behind me and met Aaries in the living room.
"Damn sis, you could've knocked."
"Since when do I do that?"
"My point exactly. You need to start knocking."
"Why Rain? Were you busy?" she asked me looking me up and down. She studied my body language and noticed that my hair was in total disarray. There was a difference in wet hair that had just been shampooed and wet hair that had

been rolling around in a bed and she knew it. Plus my eyes told it all and I couldn't hide it.

Aaries'eyes got big as she began to figure out what I was up to. You got company?"

All I could do was sit there and smile. Aaries' mouth flew open and she began to wonder who it was. Then she frowned when she thought it might be Jack.

"It's not Jack, is it?" she demanded with her arms crossed.

"No it's not Jack. Besides I had to get rid of him, he was too clingy."

"Good, then who is it?"

I became too mysterious for her and she ran to the side door to see who's car was in the garage. Her mouth dropped when she saw Maliq's car. Then she started jumping up and down.

"See! See! I told you he had a thing for you!"

"Ssh!" I said looking back at my bedroom door wondering if Maliq could hear us.

"Hey Maliq!" she yelled loud enough to be heard - which also let him know that she approved of us being together.

"Hey Aaries," he yelled back to her.

Then Aaries put all kidding aside. She let me know that she and D were going to pick up Dominique to do another paternity test. They hadn't told Reah and didn't plan to. They were just going to pick her up, take her to the lab, and get the results back within an hour or so. They said they figured out that Reah set the whole thing up from the very beginning.

Just as we were finishing up our conversation, Aaries' cell phone rang. It was Dominic and he was outside in the hum-v to pick her up.

"I gotta go, that's D, and he's outside waiting on me. But before I go, I just want to say that I know I tease you a lot, but I'm happy for you and Maliq. You two deserve each other."

She hugged me before she left.

"Now go handle your business twin," she teased as she was walking out the door. All I could do was smile and shake my head as she exited.

# Chapter 36
# The test

Once Dominic and Aaries arrived at Reah's place, they both went to her door together. When Reah answered the door, she was a little surprised. And if looks could kill, my sister would be six feet under right now. Reah gave Aaries a look that said, 'what the hell are you doing here'. Aaries came right back with a look that let her know, that she was standing by my man. .
But Reah did a pretty good job of playing it off. She invited them in and became so sugary-sweet nice, it was sickening. Of course, this shit was all fake.
Reah called Dominique down and told her that her "father" and his wife were here to take her to a movie. When she came down stairs, she was so cute with her pink outfit, pigtails and roller shoes. She was excited and ran up to D and gave him a hug and a kiss. When he introduced her to Aaries, Dominique figured that she would give her a chance, since she seemed so nice.

Once they left, they asked Dominique what she wanted to see. She said that she wanted to see the new Shrek movie. But before they went to see the movie, they made a pit stop at a DNA lab.

Aaries and D decided that he and his daughter would take the test, go watch the movie, and then come back. They paid extra money to have the results expedited.

When they arrived back to the lab, the test results concluded exactly what Aaries and D had suspected. Reah lied about everything. Dominique was unequivocally not Dominic's daughter. Although, Aaries was happy about the results, she was not at all happy that her husband was disappointed. He had become very attached to Dominique and vice-versa. And likewise, she wasn't happy that a child would have to get her feelings hurt, but that wasn't her problem. It was Reah's. But she couldn't wait to drop Dominique off, so she could give Reah a piece of her mind.

When they arrived back to Reah's house, Reah hugged her daughter and asked her if she had fun.

"Yes, ma'am," she said as she nodded. Then she began re-enacting scenes from Shrek.

"Reah, we need to talk to you about something," Dominic told her in a way that let her know, they needed the privacy without Dominique being in ear range. Reah instructed Dominique to go to her room and to put in her favorite DVD.

Once she was in her room, Reah wanted some answers.

"So what do you have to talk to me about with her here? 'Cause she really doesn't have anything to do with Dominique," she added sarcastically.
Aaries almost interjected and lunged towards her. Dominic put his arm out as if to restrain her. "Actually, Reah, neither do I," he said as he handed her the DNA paternity results.
"Dominique is not my child."
"What? What is this?" She looked mortified. Her secret was out and she was furious.
"How dare you take my child to a place like this without my consent. I ought to sue the both of you," she said looking in Aaries' direction.
"Cut the dramatics Reah. You're much smarter than that. You may be a liar but you're not stupid," Dominic retorted.
Aaries just stood there and listened with her arms crossed. Her body stance was positioned like she was waiting to knock Reah on her ass. But she respected the fact the Dominic wanted to talk to Reah about the lies. She didn't say a word.
"All I want to know is why you lied."
All of a sudden, Aaries couldn't take it anymore. "I'll tell you why she lied. Because she thought she was going to break up our marriage. Isn't that right Reah?" she said walking toward her.
"You wanted him all to yourself, didn't you? Well too damn bad, your plan backfired on your trick ass! You are so sorry Reah. So sorry that

you had a baby by another man and tried to pin it on my husband. Then you had the nerve to name your child after my husband. So now the irony in this whole situation is that your daughter's name is going to remind you of just how stupid you are! And you ought to be ashamed, 'cause now you have to go and explain why Dominic is no longer going to be coming around. It's bitches like you that give real women a bad name."

"Yeah, Reah I thought you had more class than that."

"Shut up! Both of you, just shut up and get the hell out of my house," she said pointing her finger in Aaries' face.

"Good riddance," Aaries said excitedly.

"Come on Babe, let's go. We're not going to get any real answers from her anyway. Besides we know the truth," Dominic said on his way out.

## Chapter 37
## The kiss-off

The next morning started off okay. I had taken my shower and was sitting in my bathrobe waiting for the coffee to finish brewing when my doorbell rang. Once again, it was Jack. This time I was infuriated. The first time was a little different, but this time he's going to get cussed out, because I politely told him never to show up at my home unannounced; and he did the exact opposite of what I asked him.

I swung the door open. "You must be stuck on stupid Jack, because I specifically told you not to pop up at my house! What is your problem?"
He looked pathetic. He looked like he hadn't bothered to shave in a couple of days and I could tell he hadn't had a hair cut in a while, either. And he had on a loose fitting jogging suit, something I had never seen him in before.
"Rain, I'm sorry. I just can't help it. I can't get you out of my mind. Can I just come inside to talk to you for a minute? I promise it'll only take a minute and then I'll get out of your hair and I won't bother you anymore."
"No Jack. Whatever you have to say, you can say it right here."

"Rain, I'm in love with you and I know you love me too. I can feel it."
All of a sudden, I had become afraid of Jack, not because of what he said but how he looked when he said it. He had this far out crazed look in his eyes. And he came out of the blue with his little "theory". But the best thing you can do when you're afraid is to not let it show.
"Well let me clear something up for you Jack. I don't love you and I never will."
"Yes you do," he said with hatred in his eyes.

He grabbed my face and tried to kiss me, but I kept turning my head so our mouths didn't touch. I slapped him and he pulled me closer to him and began groping me through my bathrobe. Instead of trying to get free from his grip, since he was much stronger than I was, I took my hands and slapped him in his ears so they would ring; and then I began yelling. It's loud and painful. It stuns your opponent long enough for you to get away. I learned this many years ago during my martial arts classes. Once I did that he immediately grabbed his ears and I took that opportunity to push him out the door. But he only fell backwards and his feet were still in the way. Just as I was about to stomp on his ankles, Maliq came from the bedroom in nothing but some pajama bottoms. He had spent the night.

"Rain what's wrong? I could hear you yelling when I was in the shower."
At the same time he was asking the question, Jack got up off the ground and limped backwards a little.
"It's Jack," I said. "He's disillusioned and I told him that I have no feelings for him."
"Move out the way," Maliq told me.
"Let me tell you something Jack. Whatever you thought you had with Rain, it's over. Rain is my woman now, you got that?!"
"You don't know how to deal with a real woman like Rain; and you certainly can't afford her like I can."
"Well I know you thought that you could buy her, but that's not the type of woman she is. I know her inside and out and she can't be bought. She's not that kind of woman. She likes the simple things, but you wouldn't know a thing about that. Now I'm going to tell you once, so listen good. Leave Rain alone! Don't come by here anymore or you're gonna have some serious problems and before you ask, yes that's a threat."
I was behind him thinking, *hell yeah, that's right Baby, you tell him.*
"I'll leave," Jack said backing away. "But both of you are going to regret how you've treated me. A person like me is better off as your ally, rather than your enemy. You'll soon find out what I'm

talking about. You're going to wish that you were much nicer to me Rain, and you too Maliq. Goodbye for now." He walked away with a smirk on his face.

As soon as he was gone, Maliq wanted me to call the police. I called them; and they refused to take a report. They said there was nothing they could do if the perpetrator was no longer at my residence. That figures. Police aren't good for shit anyway. The only time they show up is if someone is dead.

# Chapter 38
# The plot

Jack was infuriated by the way Maliq and I treated him. But he had some tricks up his sleeve unbeknownst to us. Once he got back home, he took an old pipe from his basement and he began to smash whatever was in sight.

"Who the hell does she think she is," Jack yelled. "She's going to wish that she never met me. She doesn't know who she's dealing with. That's alright! That's alright! I got something for her and her beloved Maliq too," he said grinning like a Cheshire cat.

He ran back upstairs to his living room and grabbed a pen and paper. He began making a list. *Pliers, wrench, sodium hydroxide, butcher knife, and one pack of chicken. Yeah, this ought to do the trick,* he thought.

After he changed clothes into some khaki cargo pants and a polo shirt, he gathered a large burlap bag along with a butcher knife and his briefcase. The first place he went to was a home improvement store. He bought a pair of pliers, a wrench, and some sodium hydroxide. Sodium hydroxide is a caustic chemical agent used to clear one's drain. Then he shot across town and went to an all-purpose store and purchased a butcher knife. And finally before his crazed attempts at revenge, he went to the grocery store to purchase a pack of chicken.

Once he had everything he needed, a few hours had passed, he thought he'd head back towards my house. I wasn't home, but then Jack knew that and that was exactly what he was waiting for, an opportunity to get into my house while I was away. Everything he did was thought out very carefully. Once again, he parked around the block and walked the remainder of the way to my house. He never wanted to take a chance that Aaries or Dominic might be home. Jack made sure he had some of his supplies with him. He took his briefcase with the butcher knife in it and a pack of chicken in a plastic bag. When he finally made it to the back door, he did the same as before. He unlocked the door with my key and decoded the alarm. He placed the chicken in the sink and began with his inquisitiveness before he went on with his mastermind plan. He began rummaging through my things - my clothes, jewelry, my mail, everything. As he was doing that, he heard a key go through my front door. He grabbed his briefcase and hid behind my bedroom door with the butcher knife ready for something, anything to pop off. He heard a voice. It was Aaries and she was on her cell. Apparently, she was looking for something specific, but couldn't find it. And she was so engrossed into her phone call that she was oblivious to the fact that my alarm wasn't set. I always set my alarm and she knew it. And she didn't go into the kitchen; otherwise she would've seen the chicken sitting in the sink. Aaries was in and out within less than five minutes.

Jack was glad that he didn't have to hurt her, but he would have if he had too. Now since Aaries had left, he decided to hurry up and do what he came to do. He called out to my kitten.

"Here kitty, kitty, kitty. Oh pretty kitty, where are you?"

Mink had been asleep under my bed when Jack called for her. As soon as Mink saw Jack, she began hissing just like the first time. She was in attack mode. Jack decided to win her affection temporarily. He went into the kitchen and cut open the chicken and held it out for Mink to smell. As soon as she walked toward him with the chicken, Jack grabbed her, then the butcher knife. What he did next was unbelievable.

# Chapter 39
# Jack-in-the-box

I had such a long day that I decided to leave work early. Maliq and I decided we would just chill out and watch a movie at my place. We picked up a movie and some Thai food and headed to my place. As soon as we walked in through the front door, I knew something was wrong immediately. My alarm didn't go off. We walked in a little further. I kept the door open, just in case someone was in my house. When I walked into the kitchen, I noticed that the back door was open. Jack had purposely left the door unlocked and open. He had become brazen and wanted me to know that it was him. I immediately picked up the phone in the kitchen and called the police. Then I yelled and told Maliq that someone had broken in. He continued to check the living room and the closets to make sure no one was there. After I hung up the phone I turned around and I couldn't believe what I saw in the sink. There was a tiny, bloody heart, liver, and other organs with blood covering it and a knife stabbed through it. And there was a note attached to it. The note read: *Rain you ripped my heart out, now I rip out yours…Meow, meow!!*

As soon as I read the note I let out a blood curdling scream and I began hyperventilating. Maliq had been checking the other rooms in the house and found nothing. He came running into the kitchen to see what was wrong with me.

"What's wrong Rain!" He came running into the kitchen with the Louisville Slugger I kept for protection. I had begun crying uncontrollably. And all I could do was point to the note and the knife. This was absolutely sick. Jack was sick! How could I have been so wrong about him and not see any of this coming.

"That sick bastard killed Mink! He killed my cat!"

Maliq immediately took me into his arms to comfort me. As we were waiting for the police to arrive, we could hear something moving in my bedroom. It sounded like someone was scratching at the walls.

"Maliq, I thought you said you checked the bedroom out and that the coast was clear."

"I did. Wait here Rain."

As Maliq went to check out the noise and scratches, the police had arrived and took my statement and dusted the doorknob for fingerprints and they took pictures of everything. When Maliq came back into the kitchen, he had a smile on his face and Mink in his arms.

"Mink," I said running to give my cat the biggest squeeze ever.

"That son of a bitch just wanted you to think that he killed Mink. What he really did was had her hidden in the hamper and she was trying to claw her way out of it. As soon as I walked into the room, she began meowing."

"That son of a bitch is gonna pay for all of this!" The excitement of all the people in the house had scared Mink, so she jumped out of my arms and ran back into the bedroom.

After the police came, they had called for a forensic pathologist, since they thought that Mink was killed. She said that it indeed was from an animal, but not from a cat. Apparently, it was giblets from a chicken; and he wanted me to think it all came from Mink.

As the police were wrapping everything up, they let me know that there was no sign of forced entry. Whoever had come in had a key. And there was no doubt in my mind that it was Jack. But the question remains, how did he get a key? Either way, I knew I was going to have to change my locks. And I'd have to get a restraining order.

As soon as the police left, Maliq wanted me to pack my things and spend the night at his house.

"No, I'm not going to let him scare me up out of my own house. I'm staying right here."

"Rain, at least until you can get these locks changed. Or you can crash at Aaries' place."
"No Maliq, because then he'll think he won. I'm staying in the comfort of my own home. I'll just be sure to set the alarm, so I'll know if he tries to come back."
"Well, I'll stay with you. And tomorrow I'll change the locks for you. And another thing, you need to get a restraining order on Jack first thing tomorrow morning."
"I am. I had already planned on it."
"Good, now I need you to tell me where he lives."
"No Maliq, you're not going over there. Don't you know by now, that fool is crazy? He's a psychopath!"
"I know, but a good ass whippin' won't hurt him."

Once all the commotion died down, Maliq had made me a cup of tea. We relaxed on the couch and tried to watch a movie. All I could do was think about how deranged Jack was. As I was doing that, my phone rang and it was Aaries. She said she felt like something wasn't right with me. I filled her in on all the details and told her that I wasn't alone. Maliq was taking good care of me. She was calling me from her cell phone and she said she and Dominic would be right over before they went home. They wanted to check on me.

When they arrived, it was simply a bunch of hugs and kisses. Dominic even asked me if I wanted him to handle it. Even though he's straight laced now, he still had plenty of contacts that were still in the streets. At one time in his life, the street was all he knew. His friend Barren could easily arrange for anyone to disappear, all I had to do was say the word.

I told him no and that I would handle this the right way. And the first thing tomorrow morning, 'd be at the courthouse to get a restraining order.

## Chapter 40
## The champ is here

The next day, I immediately got the restraining order. It was all I could think about. It was pretty much an all day process that was just a bunch of paper pushing; but hopefully it would do the trick and show Jack that I meant business. They told me Jack would be served that very same day. Not to mention, I didn't want any more run-ins between him and Maliq. And since I had been gone so long from the restaurant, I decided that when I went in that day, I would stay until late. Normally I left around six or seven, but tonight would be different. Once I arrived at the restaurant, the lot was so full. It was so busy that cars were parked across the street in the next parking lot. I walked in and discovered everything was in full swing. It was close to three-thirty in the afternoon when I arrived. And although it was a late arrival for me, the rest of the day seemed to zip by. Wil was holding down a bar full of happy-hour socialites and Aaries handled her business with our record keeping. She finally left around seven o'clock. Since she and Dominic had reconciled, they were spending a

lot more time with each other. By the time eleven o'clock rolled around, I was exhausted.
"Why don't you go on home Rain? You know I'll make sure everything is locked up and taken care of." Wil noticed that I had been yawning as I was placing the chairs on top of the tables for the floors to be mopped. There were only a few of my employees that I had trusted and he was one of them. I knew I could count on him. I smiled and thanked him and then headed on out. My feet hurt so badly; it seemed like an eternity to walk across the street and half way across the parking lot. Once I got to my car, I cranked the engine to let my car warm up briefly. I was so exhausted that I leaned forward, closed my eyes and let my forehead lie on the steering wheel. When I was ready to pull off, I looked in my rearview mirror and was horrified by what I saw. It was Jack staring at me in the backseat and he was angry. I screamed and immediately tried to jump out. I managed to get the door open but Jack pulled my ponytail and prevented me from getting out of the car.

"What is your problem Rain? You really didn't have to do this," he said with the restraining order in his right hand. And do you think a little piece of paper is going to keep me from you if I really want to see you bitch? Huh?"

All I could do was scream and I tried to reach back and scratch his hand, but he hung on for dear life. When that didn't work, I laid on the horn in hopes that someone would hear me and see me and more importantly help me. That seemed to work, because he tried to grab at my hands to keep me from making more noise. He let go of my hair for a brief second - long enough for me to get away; and I ran back towards the restaurant. Jack ran after me. When I got to the front door, I realized that I left my keys in the car with the car running. I banged on the glass in hopes that Wil would hear me. "Wil, open up! Help me, its Rain," I screamed out to him. I turned back around and noticed Jack was getting closer, but suddenly something happened. As Jack ran into the street, a car came around the corner and side swiped him. It wasn't a deadly hit, but just enough to render a person unconscious. The next thing I knew, the car screeched and stopped; and the person got out to see if Jack was all right. By this time, Wil had opened the door and saw that I was visibly shaken. He asked me what happened and I told him that I had a restraining order on Jack and what he had done in the car.

"I'm calling the police," he said. As he was doing this, I peeked out the window to see if Jack was still down. But to my surprise, I found nothing…No car, no driver and most importantly, no Jack. He had disappeared without a trace. When the police arrived, they said that there was nothing that they could do, because Jack wasn't even there, let alone a crime even being committed. Jack, although stunned from being hit in the leg, managed to limp to his car and get out of dodge before the police arrived. He convinced the driver that he was all right and told her not to call the police. Once Jack arrived back to his house, he parked his car and slowly limped his way to his front door. As he tried to unlock it, he dropped his keys. He struggled to pick them up, because he was in pain; but when he managed to straighten his body out and tried the lock again, someone tapped him on the shoulder. When Jack turned around, all he saw was a flying fist to his nose. He fell backwards and grabbed at his nose. He noticed it was bleeding. He tried to get up, but Maliq hovered over him and kept pounding his face in. Jack couldn't get any licks in.

"You're going to stay away from Rain, you sick bastard. And if I even find out that you're even thinking about coming near her, there's more where this is coming from. In fact, I'm going to give you something worse that what you just got."

Jack was disheveled and he had the wind knocked out of him. "You will regret this Maliq.

Mark my words," he said through a swollen eye, bloody nose and a bloody fat lip.

Jack grabbed him by his collar. "I'm not worried about your threats. Just stay away from Rain," he said as he walked out of Jack's house. Maliq remembered a conversation we had a while back. I told him the name of Jack's subdivision and that he lived off of Sugarloaf Parkway. He was determined to find Jack and simply kept driving around. He noticed Jack's car, but wasn't sure until he saw Jack get out of the car. I guess Maliq loves him so me.

## Chapter 41
## Master plan

After Maliq beat Jack's ass, Jack decided to let things "die down" a little before he made his next move. He knew we would be expecting something crazy to happen. And just after about two weeks, just when we thought the restraining order had done it's trick, that's when Jack decided to come from back up out of the woodworks.

This particular morning, Jack woke up extremely early, 4am to be exact. He knew where Maliq lived, but now he wanted to know where he worked. He planned on driving to his house, parking right down the street from his house and then following him to work. He wanted to be up early, because he had no idea what time Maliq left his house for work. He figured even if he had to be at work by 6am, Jack would definitely be at his house by 5am and await his departure. Jack needed to be able to mix in most crowds, so as not to be recognized. He decided to wear regular slacks and a polo type shirt with a baseball cap. Jack also drove the Lexus so that his BMW would not be recognized.

Once he arrived at Maliq's house, he just sat in the car and plotted all the things he planned on doing today. One hour had passed since Jack had arrived and the lights in Maliq's house had not yet come on. After the second hour, Jack dozed off to sleep. About twenty minutes later, a speeding motorcycle awakened him. Maliq must've got up between 6:30am and 6:45am. Seven fifteen rolled around and the garage door came up. Jack started the car to get ready to roll. Jack noticed that Maliq seemed a little rushed today. He was even speeding out of the subdivision. Once they got on the main streets, Jack made sure to leave at least one car in between them, so Maliq wouldn't suspect he was being followed. About almost an hour later, Maliq rode up into a federal building with several levels of parking. It seemed that Maliq didn't have to work today; he had a court hearing about his son. After he parked, he rushed in and that gave Jack ample opportunity to accomplish what he came for. He got up under Maliq's car and took his pliers and cut a portion of his brake line. The reason he cut only a portion of it was because when Maliq drove off, he would only have a small fender bender if he were to hit something on his way out of the parking lot. No, what Jack wanted was more devious, deadly even. He only cut a part of the brake line, so that he could pour sodium hydroxide in it and it would slowly eat away at the remainder of the brake line. So as

Maliq is driving he won't notice it right away. In fact, he wouldn't notice it until it's too late. That's exactly what Jack wanted. He wanted Maliq dead.

# Chapter 42
# Up in smoke

Jack was feeling real good right about now. He was on cloud nine. But he felt like he needed or rather wanted to do more. Immediately after tampering with Maliq's car, he went straight over to Lena's. When he arrived, he parked in an inconspicuous area, and just as he was about to get out of his car and approach the restaurant, Wil had come out back for one of his numerous cigarette breaks. Jack had studied him several times and learned of his patterns. Wil was simple, a creature of habit. He took a smoke break about every couple of hours and he always stood out back behind the restaurant. Jack even went, at one time, to take notice of his cigarette brand…Newports. There had been several butts near the dumpster. As Wil was smoking, he stepped to the side of the restaurant and thought he caught a glimpse of Jack's car behind another vehicle. Jack had ducked down in his seat so he wouldn't be spotted. Wil stared for a moment and then decided it wasn't Jack. He thumped the cigarette butt to the ground and made sure it was completely out by putting it out with his shoe; then he went back inside. After Wil went back inside,

Jack waited for a few more minutes before approaching the back of the restaurant. He got out of his car and looked very suspicious, as he as trying to make his way over to the back door of Lena's. Just as he was making it across the street, Wil came back out. He didn't trust Jack and wanted to be sure that indeed the car was not Jack's. When Wil got outside and looked in that direction, he and Jack spotted each other. They both immediately froze in their tracks and their eyes locked briefly. And just as Wil suspected, there was Jack in plain sight, headed for the restaurant. Jack made a run for it, but Wil had already run back inside. Wil ran to the closest phone, which was on the side where the kitchen was located. There was an old phone mounted on the wall and he immediately dialed 911.
"911. State your emergency."
"I would like to report a stalker, his name is…"
The next thing Wil knew was that he was being strangled by the cord of the same phone he was trying to use. Jack had made it into the back door. And unbeknownst toWil, he didn't realize that he had not pulled the door up far enough to catch the lock. So, before Jack went in, he peeked in down the hallway to see if there would be any surprises waiting on him. Once he thought the coast was clear, he crept up into the kitchen and overheard Wil speaking to the operator. He immediately

became enraged and double wrapped the phone cord around Wils' neck until he saw his eyes roll to the top of his head. His eyes had also become bloodshot, which is a common occurrence when being deprived of oxygen. And all the while, Wil was gasping for air and making choking noises. Then suddenly he seemed to stop breathing and fell to the ground. Before Jack left, he checked Wil's pockets and pulled out a pack of his cigarettes, ran out and peeked down the hallway again; then once the coast was clear, he ran out the back door. Jack pulled a lighter from his pants pocket, lit the cigarette and then threw it in a laundry basket full of towels that were sitting in the back hallway. Jack knew exactly what he was doing. When the fire rescue team and police arrived, he wanted it to appear accidental, not arson. Jack ran all the way back to his car; and when he got in his car, he peeled out and began talking out loud to himself.

"They don't know me. I told 'em! I told 'em! Especially that Maliq...They fucked with the wrong one.

.

## Chapter 43
## *Ish* hit the fan

When I got home, I called down to Aaries' house and told her what had been going on with Jack and I and how Maliq ended up getting involved as well.

"There's got to be something more that we can do Rain. We have to stop this fool, 'cause he is really crazy!"

"I know Aaries. I already got the restraining order on him, but besides, just like the police said, there's nothing that they can do unless they actually see him in the act of committing a crime."

"Well, I told you a long time ago to go ahead and get some surveillance installed inside and outside the restaurant, but no, you want to be cheap about the whole thing."

"So what are you saying? It's my fault Jack wasn't caught?" "You're the one who knows how to pick 'em Rain."

"Whatever! Look if that's all you got to say, then I gotta go," I told her as I slammed down the phone.

No sooner than I hung up on Aaries, my home phone rang. I thought it was her calling back. When I looked at the caller id, it was Brady hospital. They were calling to tell me that Maliq was in a car accident. I immediately felt all the blood rush from my body and I felt cold. I hate to say it, but I immediately thought the worse. My heart sank.

"Is he ok?" I asked with tears welling up in my eyes.

"He's alright. We had to admit him. He's in stable condition, but he's heavily sedated. All he kept asking for was Rain Hunter."

"I'm on my way." Before I left, I called Aaries back and told her what happened. She offered to drive.

When we arrived, they let both of us into his room. Dominic made it a few minutes later. Aaries had called him while we were on the way. Surprisingly, Maliq was awake. The doctor let us know that all he suffered was a broken arm. Apparently, when his brakes wouldn't work, he tried not to panic and let the passenger side of his car scrape up against the median to try and slow down and eventually stop. Well, instead he went a little too much to the right; and the median clipped the front a little too much; and because of the speed the car was going, it made Maliq flip over and as a result, he broke his arm.

Both Aaries and I gave him a hug and a kiss. Dominic just sat and listened. And while we were talking, a police officer came in and gave

Maliq some information about his car. It wasn't totaled, but more importantly than that, they had it analyzed and after doing a little detective work, they found that someone had tampered with the brake line. They found a caustic substance commonly used in unclogging sinks on or around the brake pads. As soon as he said that, we all looked at each other.

Once the officer left, I apologized to Maliq. "It's all my fault Maliq. None of this would be happening to you if I hadn't dragged you into all of this."

"It's not your fault Rain. It's mine. This was Jack's vengeance."

"What do you mean?"

"I didn't tell you, but the day after he terrorized you with the cat incident, I found out where he lived and I hurt him pretty badly."

"Maliq, I told you to stay away from him."

Although I was glad someone was defending my honor, I didn't want him to get hurt or die in the process.

"I know, but I did what I felt I had to do."

"Rain, I told you all you have to do is say the word. There are a few people who owe me a few favors. And I can make your problem disappear," Dominic said. "Just say the word and it's done."

# Chapter 44
## When it rains in pours

About an hour after we had all been visiting Maliq in his room, Dominic and Aaries decided to give us a little privacy. They said they were going to the hospital cafeteria to get a bite to eat.

"You want anything, twin," Aaries asked me sympathetically.

"No thanks, I'm not hungry."

"Alright, D and I will be back." I nodded. As soon as they left, I gave Maliq a kiss on his right cheek and decided to cuddle up with him on that extremely small bed. I had to lay to his right side, because his left arm was the one that was broken. He didn't say much, he just smiled and kissed me back, but he kissed me on the lips. Then that passion just took over. It took over so much, I almost got up to go and lock the door, so I could handle my business. But instead, I calmed down, took a deep breath and then grabbed the remote and turned to the news. The next thing we saw shocked us. It was footage of my restaurant going up in flames.

"Oh, my God!" I said, horrified by what I was seeing. "My restaurant!" We both sat up in the bed and I grabbed the remote control and adjusted the volume. There was a female reporter covering the story. She stated that fire crews had been trying to put out the blaze for some time now, but had not yet been successful. They also stated that they believed that all customers had gotten out safely without sustaining injury. Then the camera crew focused directly on the employees. I recognized several servers, chefs, and dishwashers.

They interviewed one of my chefs and he stated that he wasn't sure if everyone got out alive or not. Then I remembered that Wil was scheduled to work earlier, but I didn't know if he had left early or not. I grabbed my cell phone out of my purse and tried to call Wil, but to no avail, I couldn't get service in the hospital. I reached to my right and grabbed the landline phone and tried again and all I got was his voice mail. I was worried and nervous and I let him know to call me as soon as he got the message. As soon as I hung up the phone, Aaries and D had come back to the room. The cafeteria had already closed for the day. Aaries noticed how frantic I was and she noticed Maliq trying and telling me to calm me down.

"Calm down for what? What's wrong guys?"

"Aaries come on we've got to get over to Lena's. There's been a fire!"

"What? What do you mean a fire? What's happened? What's going on Rain?"
"I'll tell you on the way, but Maliq and I just saw the restaurant on the news going up in smoke." I had my purse on my shoulder and immediately turned toward Maliq.
"Baby, I don't want to leave you, but I need to check this out."
"Rain, I'm fine and I'm going to be all right. Don't worry about me. Just go check on your spot and just call me here later on, once you know something."
"Ok," I said as I gave him a quick peck on the lips. Dominic had decided to drive since he knew that Aaries and I were both a little frazzled.

## Chapter 45
## This too shall pass

Once we arrived, Aaries and I both ran from the car to the police to identify ourselves as the owners and to find out what was going on. When our employees saw us, they ran up to Aaries and I and gave us a hug. We were just glad to see no one was hurt or killed. We were pleased to see that the fire rescue team had managed to put out the fire and that at least the whole restaurant had not been destroyed. There was still much to be salvaged. It seemed that only the backside of the restaurant, along with some of the roof had gotten damaged. We also learned from the police that they had recovered a body and unfortunately it was Wil. Aaries and I both covered our mouths in amazement and started to cry. Once the employees got wind of it, you could hear cries in the background and they all hugged each other in a huddle. Dominic immediately comforted his wife and I tried to suck it up through the tears as I got more details. They said that they found his body in the kitchen with a cord wrapped around his throat. He had been strangled. As the police were filling us in with the other details, the fire crew said that they had more information. They said that it was an arson fire orchestrated and disguised to look like an accident. They said the person was an amateur and tried to make it look like the fire was started by a cigarette. Aaries and I immediately looked at each other in terror. Wil was the only employee who ever went out back to smoke. The police also let us hear the 911 recording that was called in. They wanted to know if we recognized the voice. We nodded as we gasped in horror realizing that Jack had just committed murder and arson all in one night.

"Do you ladies have any idea who might have done this," the police questioned.

"Jack. Jack Anderson," I bolstered out. "I have a protection order against him and I'm sure Wil was just trying to help protect me."

The news media overheard some of the conversation and wanted to interview Aaries and I. Naturally, we obliged them.

"Ma'am, can you tell us how you feel with your place of business going up in flames?"

Aaries decided to answer. "What kind of heartless question is that? How do you think we feel? This is our family legacy, our livelihood, not to mention one of our employees and dear friend was killed." The police didn't want us divulging the name just yet, especially since they hadn't even contacted his next of kin. Other questions

just came from everywhere. And there had to be at least six or seven microphones in our faces.
"The police are calling it a murder-arson. Who would want to do something so heinous? Do you all have any ideas?"
"I'll answer that," I said. The man's name is Jack Anderson. He's a sick crazed lunatic who has become obsessed with me. I turned him down and now he's hell bent on getting his revenge. I have a restraining order against him, but he's violated it several times; yet the police claim, they can't do a thing unless they catch him in the act."
"That's right," Aaries said intervening. "The sick son-of-a-bitch is fixated on my sister and won't leave her alone." Then Aaries walked up closer to the cameras. "But Jack, I've got a message for you. Leave Rain alone! If you don't we got something for you." Then she got so angry and started cussing at the camera, D had to grab her and pull her to the side and tell her to calm down.
After a few hours of trying to get the investigation wrapped up, I was exhausted. My sister and Dominic insisted that I stay with them overnight, especially after what just happened.

## Chapter 46
## Pop goes the weasel

Some time had passed and Aaries and I were still dealing with the fire marshal as well as the insurance company. They said it would be another few weeks before we could resume business as usual.

On the home front, everything was going well with Maliq and I. He had been released from the hospital about five days after the accident; and he and I couldn't have been happier. The same could be said for Aaries and Dominic. They focused on their marriage and have become much closer to one another. In fact, so close that she and Dominic found out that they were six weeks pregnant. Aaries had gotten used to the idea, especially since she knew how happy it made her husband. He was much more doting and accommodating toward her. In other words, he spoiled the hell out of her. Yes, indeed. Everything was kosher. Even Jack had dropped out of the scene for a while. Or so it would seem. And it took everything in Maliq and Dominic, not to confront Jack. Maliq knew that would only make things worse.

On this particular day, it was a typical one for Atlanta in the summer - hot and extremely humid. In fact, Aaries decided to open her windows and the front door for air rather than run the air conditioner, since she was painting her kitchen. Shortly after she had resumed her painting, she heard the screen door open and close. "That was quick Babe. You're back already, huh, she inquired. She had her back to the kitchen entrance when she felt a presence. "You know you should really learn to lock your doors even in broad daylight." The familiar voice had a low and cold tone to it. Aaries turned around and almost fell off the stepladder she was using to paint. "What the hell do you think you're doing here?" It was Jack standing in the kitchen doorway with a smug look on his face with his arms crossed. He had been watching the house for a while and he saw Dominic drive off. "Thought I'd pay you a little visit," Jack said with a grimace on his face taking a small step toward her. "Don't you come near me," she shouted taking a small step back and looking for anything that could be used as a weapon. The cutlery set was on the counter top in between both she and Jack. Her heart was racing so fast, it made her perspire even more. "What's wrong?" You don't need to be afraid of me. I just came to have a little chat with you and deliver a message. I just want to know why you and your sister are hell bent on trying to destroy me? Huh? I mean first she gets a restraining order out on me, then she sends her little boyfriend to try and hem me up, and then the two of you slander my good name all over the news. I mean just who do you think you are?" By this time he had a frown on his face and seemed to be irrational. "Go ahead. You had so much to say on TV, what's up now? Cat got your tongue or what?" Aaries tried to measure her distance from the cutlery set and with only one entrance in the kitchen, she thought about how quickly she could make it to reach for a butcher knife. Just as she lunged toward the knives, Jack beat her to it. He reached for Aaries' right hand to stop her and pushed the knives so hard off the counter top, they fell and hit the oven on the opposite side of the kitchen. "Do you think I'm playing with you here?" he said reaching for her throat. Aaries was stunned and immediately began to gag and choke. Her emotions went from anger to fear in no time. She tried to pry Jack's hands from around her throat, but had no luck. "Let me tell you something. You and your sister need to keep my name out of your mouth. And tell Rain whenever I want her, I can have her. And no fucking restraining order can keep me away. Not even that sorry ass boyfriend can keep me away. I told her she was going to pay for everything she has done to me. As he released her neck, he walked toward the door and paused a moment, then turned around to see Aaries on the floor panting and gasping. "By the way, nice paint job." As Jack walked out she scrambled to pick herself up to lock the door and called the police. Then she called D. After that, it was on!

When Dominic found out what Jack had done to Aaries, he was livid! He could've killed Jack right then and there. The police finally arrived and took a statement, but said there was nothing they could do considering there weren't any witnesses nor was there any indication of bodily harm. This infuriated Dominic even more. After the police left, he had Aaries call me over to their house. Maliq and I had been spending some time together, so when I got the call and Aaries told me what happened, I had Maliq join us. "Rain, I need for you to tell me anything and everything about this motherfucker 'cause I got plans for him. I mean coming over here and scaring my wife like that and she's pregnant too. Nah! It's definitely going down." "I can show you where he lives D. In fact I have some unfinished business of my own with him," Maliq volunteered. "Nah, I need to deal with him on my own. Besides, I don't need any witnesses." Aaries and I just looked at each other. Maliq simply nodded his head, he knew what time it was and so did we.

It was only a matter of a couple of hours before D got over to Jack's house, his sidekick Barren met him there as well. They planned on dealing with Jack immediately. Unbeknownst and surprisingly to D, Jack had vanished without a trace. Maybe that had been a blessing in disguise, because what they had in mind had nothing at all to do with talking things out. They wanted to take it to the streets, and Barren had no qualms with canceling a motherfucker.

# Chapter 47
# The party

One month later everything seemed to be wonderful. Aaries' marriage to Dominic was better than ever, especially after she found out about her pregnancy. At first, she didn't take the news that well; but after seeing how happy it made her husband, she grew into it and now she's all for it.

And best of all, I hadn't seen or heard from Jack. I told Dominic that I didn't want Jack to be killed, because I couldn't live with that on my conscience, but I could live with Jack leaving Atlanta and never coming back. And that's exactly what happened. All I know is Dominic and Barren finally caught up with Jack after several weeks of hiding. Barren had arranged for a few of his old homies to have a chat with Jack and whatever they told him must've scared him enough to leave. The next day he had a moving company pack all of his belongings and he put his house on the market.

I was so excited, I decided to have a party. Not to mention it was Aaries' and my birthday. We were thirty years old now and wanted to do it up real big. A few ideas had crossed our minds for a theme. There had already been too many 70's parties, and then I thought of an 80's party, or even a pool party. None of that worked for us. We wanted it to be dramatic and different. We decided on a masquerade party, something similar to the movie *'eyes wide shut'* only without the freaks.

▪▪▪▪▪▪▪▪▪▪▪▪▪▪▪▪▪▪▪▪▪▪▪▪▪▪▪▪▪▪▪▪▪▪▪▪▪▪▪▪▪▪▪▪▪▪▪▪▪▪▪▪▪▪▪▪

Before the party began I decided to do something daring that I hadn't done before. I dyed my hair the same color as my sister, auburn. This was perfect and dramatic for the party. The mask I had was green with feathers and gold rhinestones. My dress was gold, as well. And I decided I would wear my hair extra wild just for the effect it would have with the mask.

By the time nine o'clock rolled around, I rushed out the house and down the street. We decided to have the party at the clubhouse. Maliq knew it would take me forever to get ready, so he got ready early enough to allow the deejay to set up. I told him I'd meet him there. Of course when I arrived, everyone was there before me. Even Aaries and Dominic beat me. Aaries' hair was exactly like mine, except her mask was yellow with silver trimming. Her dress was yellow, as well.

A couple of hours into it, everyone was eating, drinking, dancing and having the time of their lives. Aaries and I had switched dance partners for a second. I danced with D and she danced with Maliq. While I was dancing with D, I noticed someone walk in with an all black mask. He didn't seem to mingle with anyone. He just found a corner and stayed there.

I was thirsty, so we all stopped dancing for a moment. When I went over to the punch bowl, I noticed we were out of ice. I had plenty of extra bags at home in my deep freezer.

"I'll go and get a bag. I need some fresh air anyway," Aaries said.

"I'll help you," I told her.

"No, it's cool, I'll do it. Besides, I'm having cravings for ice cubes," she laughed.

"Babe, I don't want you out there by yourself. I'm going with you," Dominic insisted.

"D, it's only around the corner. I think I can manage that. I'll only be gone for a few minutes, just long enough to get the ice and come back. If I need you I got my cell phone," Aaries told him convincingly.

"Alright, he told her, lifting his mask and giving her a peck on the lips and then kissing her barely showing tummy."

Aaries grabbed her keys and she took my car, since I was the last one to park.

When I turned around to look for the man in the all black mask, I couldn't find him anywhere. He had vanished without a trace.
And I didn't think anything of it until my sister had been gone a little too long.

# Chapter 48
## Guess who?

After Aaries parked my car, she ran into the house to grab the ice. When she went inside, she pushed the door up until it was just barely cracked. She grabbed the bag of ice and tore open the plastic and grabbed a small ice cube. Her pregnancy was bringing on some strange cravings. With an ice cube in her mouth and the bag of ice in her hands, she was ready to head back to the party. When she swung the door open, she almost choked on her ice cube. Instead, it fell out of her mouth. It was Jack!

"Hello Rain. Miss me?" he questioned with a cigarette hanging out the side of his mouth.

He had learned of our party through the wire-tapping he had done to my home phone when he broke in. With my hair now being the same color as Aaries', Jack couldn't tell us apart. After all we were identical twins. He must've been oblivious to the fact that Aaries had her wedding ring on. Otherwise, he would've noticed that he had the wrong twin.

Then Aaries moved in such a way that made him think that she was about to try and throw that ice at him. Jack pulled out his gun and pointed it at her.

"I wouldn't do that if I were you," he said closing the door behind him.

He grabbed her arm and pulled her toward my bedroom. "In fact, let's take it in here." He locked the door behind him.

Aaries tried to remain calm and think of a way out of this.

"What are you going to do Jack?" she asked him sitting on the edge of the bed.

"Don't worry, Rain. I'm not going to hurt you."

Aaries looked at him suspiciously when he said that.

"I promise. I'm not going to hurt you. I'm going to kill you," Jack told her with a far away look in his eyes. He stood by the door and told her this story about not being loved as a child, especially by his mother. Then he walked toward the bed and pulled out a small bottle of lighter fluid. He began pouring it in a circle around the bed as he continued his story. He said he never even had so much as a simple birthday cake as a child. And all he ever wanted to do was be loved by his mother.

Aaries' eyes got big. She tried to remain calm and think about how to get out of the situation. All the while, still noticing that Jack still had a lit cigarette in his mouth, he was oblivious to the fact that he had not thumped any of the ashes. They were in midair, just waiting to fall.

"All you women are evil, just like my mother," he said moving closer toward the door.

"Jack, I'm sorry for what your mother did or didn't do when you were young, but if you just let me out of here, I can take you to get some help," she told him trying to use psychology on him.

It must've been working too, because his whole demeanor changed. His face softened a little.

"Let me help you, Jack."

"But what about Maliq?"

"Don't worry, I'll leave him to be with you. Come on, we can go away right now," she said easing herself carefully off of the bed walking toward Jack. "I promise Jack. You can trust me."

Just as she said those words, Jack could hear his mother saying those very words years ago. He grabbed his head and spun around.

"No! I can't trust anything any of you say." He pointed the gun back at her and told her to back up. "You're a liar! You're not planning on leaving Maliq. I see you two are married now, and if I can't have you, I'm gonna make sure no one else does," he said lunging toward her and grabbing her wrist.

Meanwhile, Mink was under my bed and came out swinging. She hissed at him then jumped up on his shoulders and attacked his face.

Somehow Jack managed to get Mink's claw out of his neck and threw her down. She hissed again and then ran back underneath the bed. In the process, Jack dropped the gun. Aaries had picked it up and told him to back up away from the door.

She opened the door and began backing out and trying to get away from this freak. As she was backing away, the back of her dress was long and she tripped over it causing her to fall. Jack lunged forward and tried to take the gun from her. As the two struggled, Jack's cigarette fell out of his mouth. First two shots rang out! The next shot rang out. Then there was silence.

# Chapter 49
# Aftermath

By the time Dominic, Maliq, and I got to the house, it was up in flames. My screams were blood-curdling enough to send chills through one's whole body. The police and the fire department were pulling up shortly after we arrived. One of the neighbors had called them before we were able to. "Aaries!" Dominic yelled at the top of his lungs, as well. He couldn't fathom the loss of his wife, just like I couldn't fathom the loss of my sister. He ran toward the door and tried to kick it in. It took several police officers and fire rescue crew to keep him from going in to save Aaries.

Maliq tried to hold and console me, but I became so uncontrollable that I began hyperventilating. The paramedics had to sit me down and give me oxygen. Maliq sat with me. By this time, all the neighbors had come outside to see what was going on. And after it was all said and done, it looked like the fire was out completely. The fire was contained to only one part of the house. The fire rescue team had come out with a body on a stretcher and another person came out with Mink in his arms. She was fine.

When Jack opened the door, she was able

to run from under the bed down the staircase. She hid in another part of the house. I immediately snatched off my oxygen mask. Dominic, Maliq and I ran towards them. "Well, what can you tell us? Did you find my wife?" The team all looked at each other and then at us. The silence was killing me. "Well? Is my sister going to be okay or what?" The chief detective decided to finally answer. "Ma'am, this is still under investigation and we'll have information for you soon. And please, we can't have any of you in the crime scene area." "Come on Rain," Maliq gestured as he took Mink from one of the men. Dominic followed, as well. We all sat on the curb and waited for them to come and tell us something.

When they finally did give us some information, we were all stunned by what we heard. Aaries was found with a single gunshot wound to the chest. The gunshot wound was not fatal to her, but rather she died from smoke inhalation. They also found other blood splatters on the wall near the door and had brought a blood splatter expert out to the crime scene, along with the forensics team. They were able to test the DNA and found that the blood belonged to Jack. Apparently during the struggle, Aaries shot him twice and Jack was able to get the gun away from her and shot her, as well. After hearing this news, I began to sob uncontrollably into Maliq's shoulders as he tried to embrace me. Dominic, on the other hand, began to swing his fists in the air the same way Cuba Gooding Jr. did in the movie Boyz in the Hood. He was livid and he didn't know what to do. "Where is Jack? That motherfucker better be dead too, or else I'm going to kill him myself!" The detective revealed that the only body they found was Aaries'. Jack's body was not found in the house. "So that motherfucker is alive? Oh, he will be found, he will be found."

During the next couple of years, a lot happened. I was able to reflect on a lot of things. I had finally come to terms with my twins' death. I've been in therapy for quite some time, as well. Not only had I been mourning her death but I felt a sense of guilt, because it should've been me that was killed, not her. Aaries loved me so much that she died for me. She never revealed to Jack that she was really Aaries.

And to this very day, I feel guilty for that, because I lost a sister and a niece or a nephew and Dominic lost his wife and his child. I know they say things happen for a reason, but I sure can't think of any logical reason why my sister had to die like that. Maybe one day I will, but for now, I just live life to the fullest with my husband. Oh yeah, Maliq and I got married and we have a son.

His name is Aaron and how we came up with his name should be obvious.

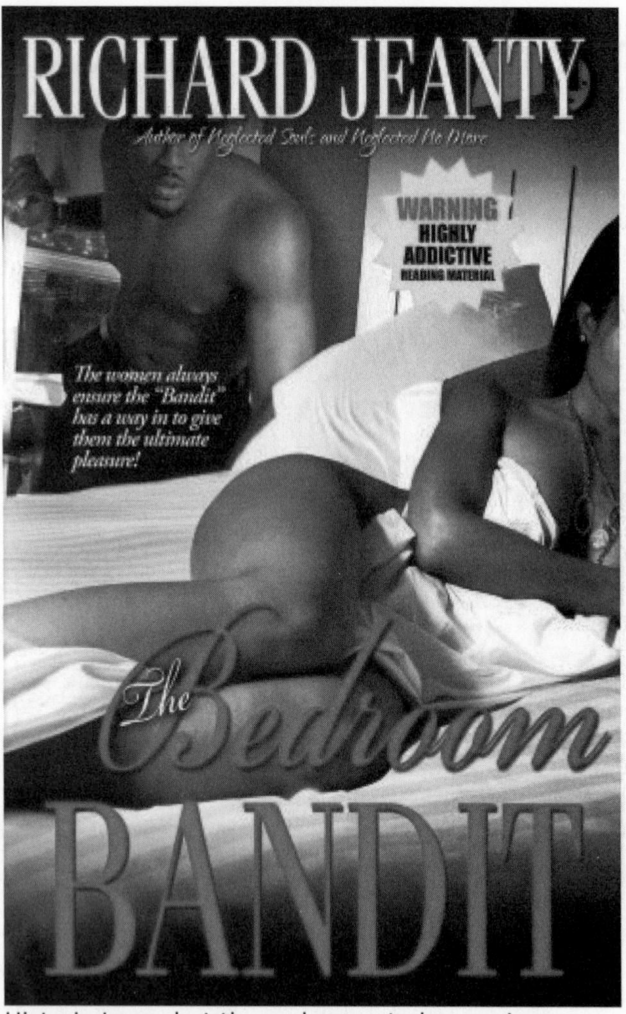


It may not be Histeria Lane, but these desperate housewives are fed up with their neglecting husbands. Their sexual needs take precedence over the millions of dollars their husbands bring home every year to keep them happy in their affluent neighborhood. While their husbands claim to be hard at work, these wives are doing a little work of their own with the bedroom bandit. Is the bandit swift enough to evade these angry husbands?

In Stores!!

**NEGLECTED SOULS**

Motherhood and the trials of loving too hard and not enough frame this story...The realism of these characters will bring tears to your spirit as you discover the hero in the villain you never saw coming... Neglected Souls is a gritty, honest and heart-stirring story of hope and personal triumph set in the ghettos of Boston.

**In Stores!!!**

Jimmy and Nina continue to feel a void in their lives because they haven't a clue about their genealogical make-up. Jimmy falls victims to a life threatening illness and only the right organ donor can save his life. Will the donor be the bridge to reconnect Jimmy and Nina to their biological family? Will Nina be the strength for her brother in his time of need? Will they ever find out what really happened to their mother?

**In Stores!!!**

Betrayal, lust, lies, murder, deception, sex and tainted love frame this story... Julian Stevens lacks the ambition and freak ability that Miko looks for in a man, but she married him despite his flaws to spite an ex-boyfriend. When Miko least expects it, the old boyfriend shows up and ready to sweep her off her feet again. She wants to have her cake and eat it too. While Miko's doing her own thing, Julian is determined to become everything Miko ever wanted in a man and more, but will he go to extreme lengths to prove he's worthy of Miko's love? Julian Stevens soon finds out that he's capable of being more than he could ever imagine as he embarks on a journey that will change his life forever.

**In Stores!!!**

The police in New York and other major cities around the country are increasingly victimizing black men. The violence has escalated to deadly force, most of the time without justification. In this controversial book, noted author Richard Jeanty, tackles the problem of police brutality and the unfair treatment of Black men at the hands of police in New York City and the rest of the country.

**In Stores!!!**

Just when Darren thinks his relationship with Tina is flourishing, there is yet another hurdle on the road hindering their bliss. Tina saw a therapist for months to deal with her sexual addiction, but now Darren is wondering if she was ever treated completely. Darren has not been taking care of home and Tina's frustrated and agrees to a break-up with Darren. Will Darren lose Tina for good? Will Tina ever realize that Darren is the best man for her?

**In Stores!!**

Ronald Murphy was a player all his life until he and his best friend, Myles, met the women of their dreams during a brief vacation in South Beach, Florida. Sexual Jeopardy is story of trust, betrayal, forgiveness, friendship and hope.

**In Stores!!!**

Tina develops an insatiable sexual appetite very early in life. She only loves her boyfriend, Darren, but he's too far away in college to satisfy her sexual needs.
Tina decides to get buck wild away in college
Will her sexual trysts jeopardize the lives of the men in her life?

**In Stores!!!**

Faith Jones, a woman in her mid-thirties, has given up on ever finding love again until she met her son's best friend, Darius. Faith Jones is walking a thin line of betrayal against her son for the love of Darius. Will Faith allow her emotions to outweigh her common sense?

**In Stores!!!**

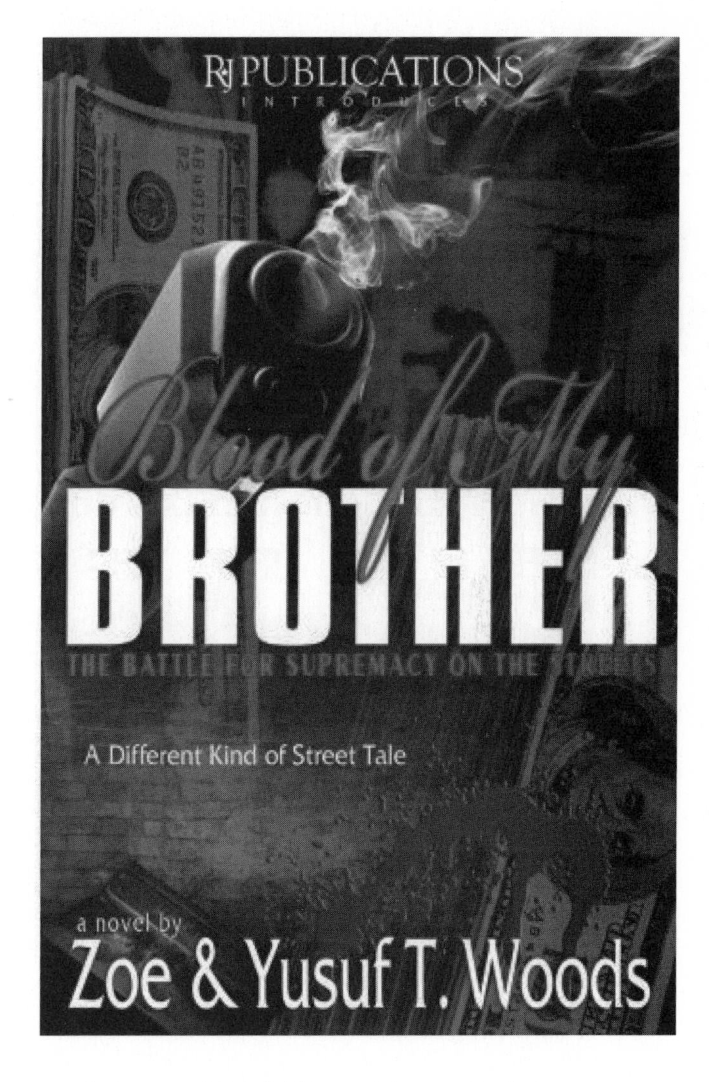


Roc was the man on the streets of Philadelphia, until his younger brother decided it was time to become his own man by wreaking havoc on Roc's crew without any regards for the blood relation they share. Drug, murder, mayhem and the pursuit of happiness can lead to deadly consequences. This story can only be told by a person who has lived it.

**In Stores!!!**

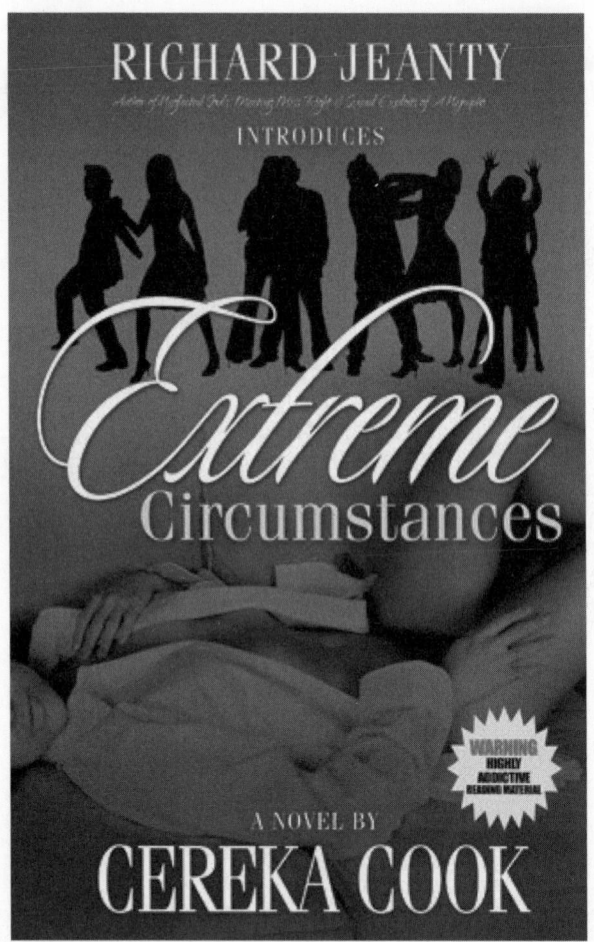


What happens when a devoted woman is betrayed? Come take a ride with Chanel as she takes her boyfriend, Donnell, to circumstances beyond belief after he betrays her trust with his endless infidelities. How long can Chanel's friend, Janai, use her looks to get what she wants from men before it catches up to her? Find out as Janai's gold-digging ways catch up with and she has to face the consequences of her extreme actions.

**In Stores!!!**

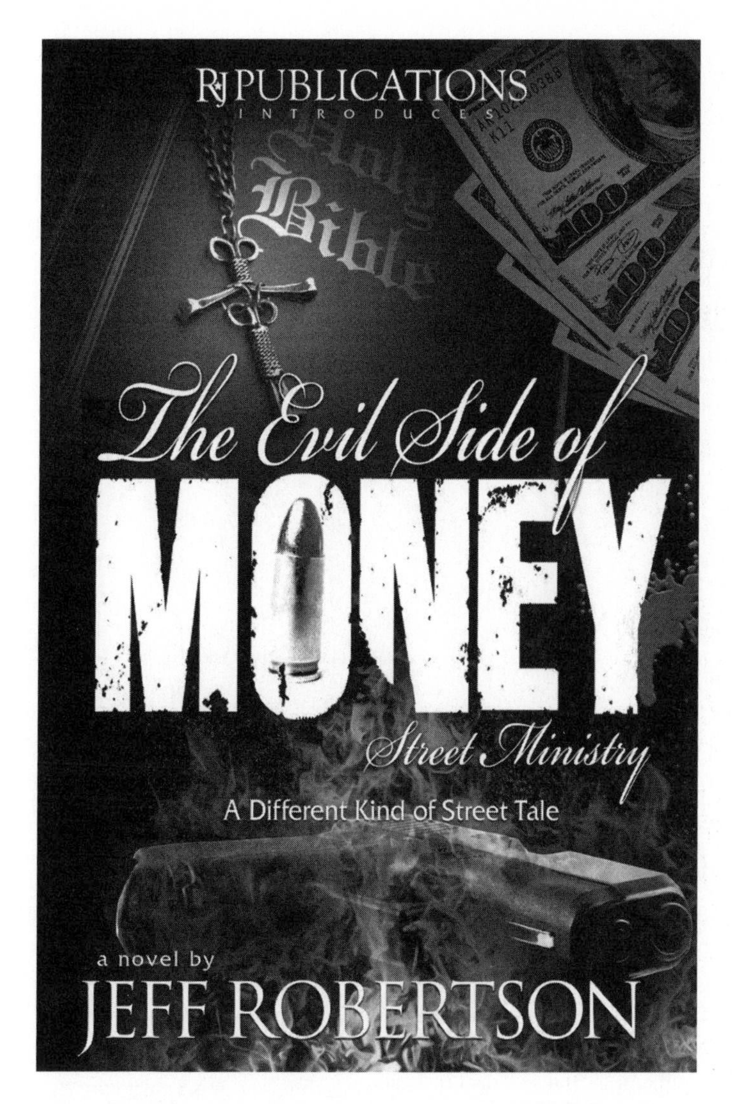


Violence, Intimidation and carnage are the order as Nathan and his brother set out to build the most powerful drug empires in Chicago. However, when God comes knocking, Nathan's conscience starts to surface. Will his haunted criminal past get the best of him?

**In Stores!!**

Yasmina witnessed the brutal murder of her parents at a young age at the hand of a drug dealer. This event stained her mind and upbringing as a result. Will Yamina's life come full circle with her past? Find out as Yasmina's crew, The Platinum Chicks, set out to make a name for themselves on the street.

**In stores!!**

Ashland's mother, Bianca, fights hard to suppress the truth from her daughter because she doesn't want her to marry Jordan, the grandson of an ex-lover she loathes. Ashland soon finds out how cruel and vengeful her mother can be, but what price will Bianca pay for redemption?

**In stores!!**

Malcolm is a wealthy virgin who decides to conceal his wealth From the world until he meets the right woman. His wealthy best friend, Dexter, hides his wealth from no one. Malcolm struggles to find love in an environment where vanity and materialism are rampant, while Dexter is getting more than enough of his share of women. Malcolm needs develop self-esteem and confidence to meet the right woman and Dexter's confidence is borderline arrogance.

Will bad boys like Dexter continue to take women for a ride?

Or will nice guys like Malcolm continue to finish last?

**In Stores!!!**

What happens when a woman's devotion to her fiancee is tested weeks before she gets married? What if her fiancee is just hiding behind the veil of ministry to deceive her? Find out as Sean Mitchell takes you on a journey you'll never forget into the lives of Angelica, Titus and Aurelius.

**In Stores!!**

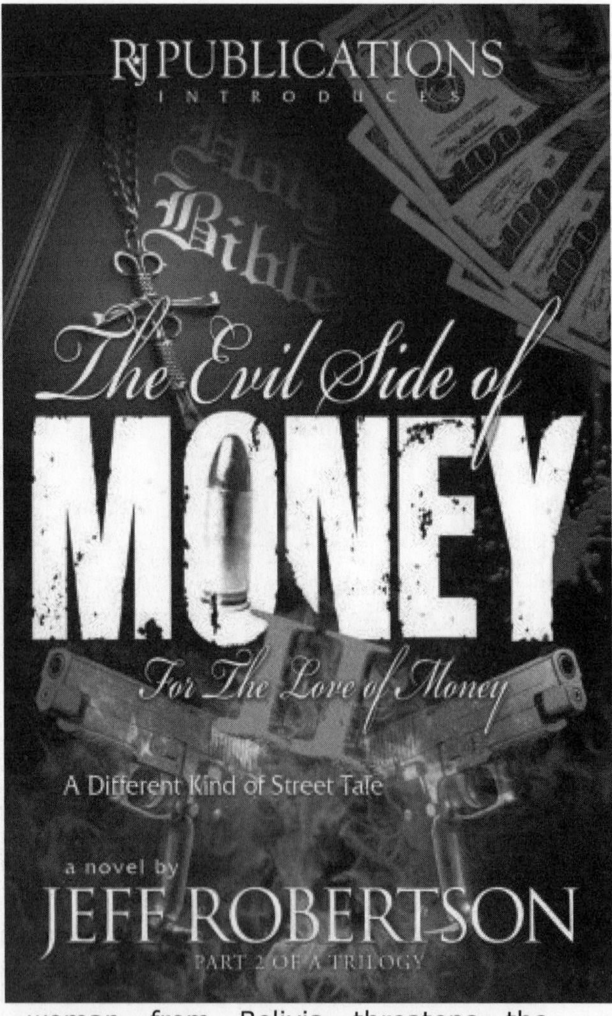


A beautigul woman from Bolivia threatens the existence of the drug empire that Nate and G have built. While Nate is head over heels for her, G can see right through her. As she brings on more conflict between the crew, G sets out to show Nate exactly who she is before she brings about their demise.

**In Stores!!!**

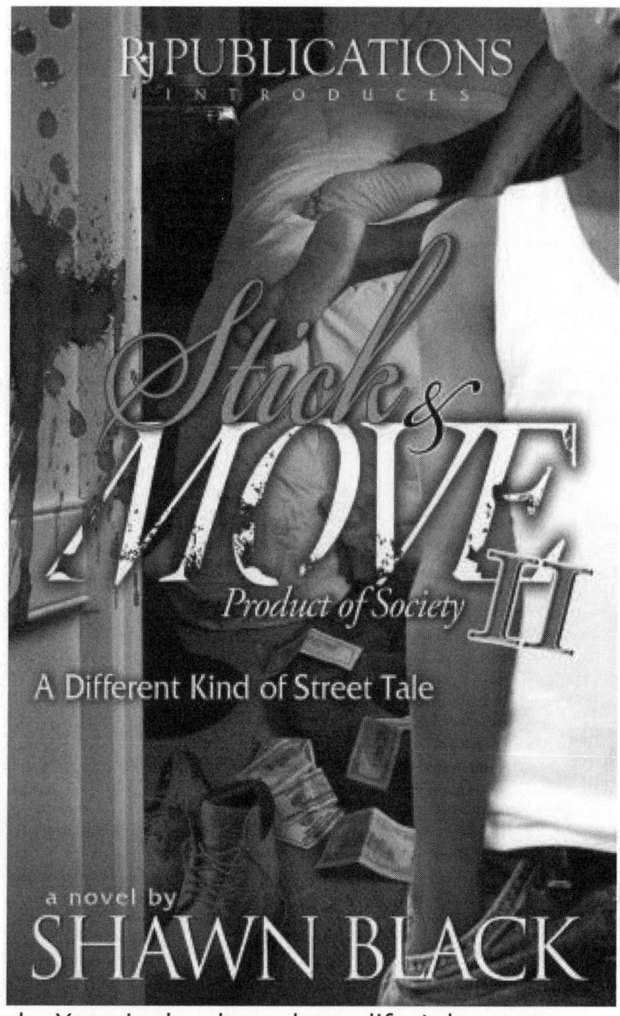


Scorcher and Yasmina's low key lifestyle was interrupted when they were taken down by the Feds, but their daughter, Serosa, was left to be raised by the foster care system. Will Serosa become a product of her environment or will she rise above it all? Her bloodline is undeniable, but will she be able to control it?

**In Stores!!**

After Chasin' Satisfaction, Miko finds that satisfaction is not all that it's cracked up to be. As a matter of fact, it left nothing but death in its aftermath. Now living the glamorous life in Miami while putting the finishing touches on his hybrid condo hotel, Julian realizes with newfound success he's now become the hunted. Julian's success is threatened as someone from his past vows revenge on him.

**Coming June 2009!!**

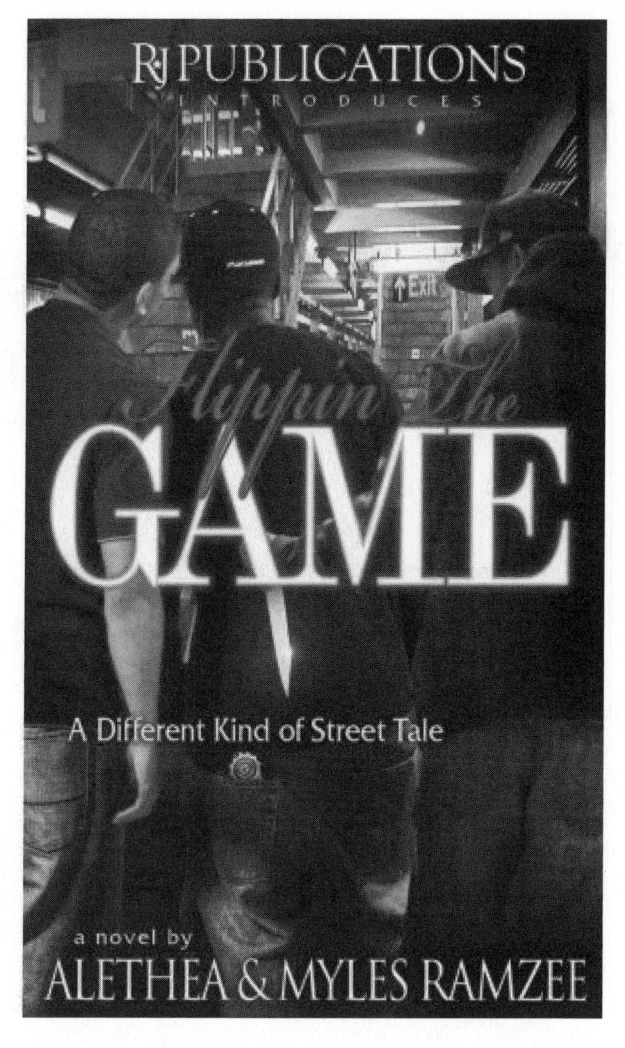


An ex-drug dealer finds himself in a bind after he's caught by the Feds. He has to decide which is more important, his family or his loyalty to the game. As he fights hard to make a decision, those who helped him to the top fear the worse from him. Will he get the chance to tell the govt. whole story, or will someone get to him before he becomes a snitch?

**In Stores!!!**

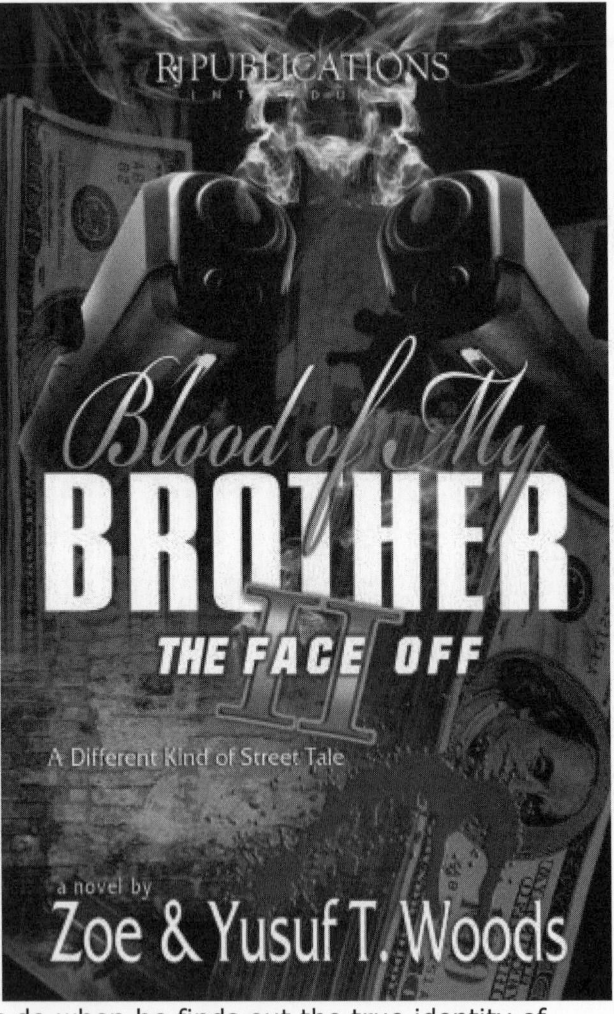


What will Roc do when he finds out the true identity of Solo? Will the blood shed come from his own brother Lil Mac? Will Roc and Solo take their beef to an explosive height on the street? Find out as Zoe and Yusuf bring the second installment to their hot street joint, Blood of My Brother.

**In Stores!!!**

When an Ex-con finds himself destitute and in dire need of the basic necessities after he's released from prison, he turns to what he knows best, crime, but at what cost? Extortion, murder and mayhem drives him back to the top, but will he stay there?

**In Stores !!!**

What happens when someone falls insanely in love? Stalking is just the beginning.

**Coming May 2009!!!**

PUBLICATIONS
BRINGING EXCITEMENT, FUN AND JOY TO READING

Use this coupon to order by mail

22. Neglected Souls, Richard Jeanty $14.95
23. Neglected No More, Richard Jeanty $14.95
24. Sexual Exploits of Nympho, Richard Jeanty $14.95
25. Meeting Ms. Right's Whip Appeal, Richard Jeanty $14.95
26. Me and Mrs. Jones, K.M Thompson ($14.95) Available
27. Chasin' Satisfaction, W.S Burkett ($14.95) Available
28. Extreme Circumstances, Cereka Cook ($14.95) Available
29. The Most Dangerous Gang In America, R. Jeanty $15.00
30. Sexual Exploits of a Nympho II, Richard Jeanty $15.00
31. Sexual Jeopardy, Richard Jeanty $14.95 Coming: 2/15/ 2008
32. Too Many Secrets, Too Many Lies, Sonya Sparks $15.00
33. Stick And Move, Shawn Black ($15.00) Coming 1/15/ 2008
34. Evil Side Of Money, Jeff Robertson $15.00
35. Cater To Her, W.S Burkett $15.00 Coming 3/30/ 2008
36. Blood of my Brother, Zoe & Ysuf Woods $15.00
37. Hoodfellas, Richard Jeanty $15.00 11/30/2008
38. The Bedroom Bandit, Richard Jeanty $15.00 March 2009
39. Stick N Move II, Shawn Black $15.00 April 2009
40. Miami Noire, W.S. Burkett $15.00 June 2009
41. Insanely In Love, Cereka Cook $15.00 May 2009
42. Blood of My Brother III, Zoe & Yusuf Woods August 2009

Name________________________________________
Address______________________________________
City________________State_____Zip Code_______

Please send the novels that I have circled above.

Shipping and Handling: Free
Total Number of Books__________
Total Amount Due______________

Buy 3 books and get 1 free. This offer is subject to change without notice.

Send institution check or money order (no cash or CODs) to:
RJ Publications
PO Box 300771
Jamaica, NY 11434

For more information please call 718-471-2926, or visit www.rjpublications.com

Please allow 2-3 weeks for delivery.

PUBLICATIONS
BRINGING EXCITEMENT, FUN AND JOY TO READING

Use this coupon to order by mail

64. Neglected Souls, Richard Jeanty $14.95
65. Neglected No More, Richard Jeanty $14.95
66. Sexual Exploits of Nympho, Richard Jeanty $14.95
67. Meeting Ms. Right's Whip Appeal, Richard Jeanty $14.95
68. Me and Mrs. Jones, K.M Thompson ($14.95) Available
69. Chasin' Satisfaction, W.S Burkett ($14.95) Available
70. Extreme Circumstances, Cereka Cook ($14.95) Available
71. The Most Dangerous Gang In America, R. Jeanty $15.00
72. Sexual Exploits of a Nympho II, Richard Jeanty $15.00
73. Sexual Jeopardy, Richard Jeanty $14.95 Coming: 2/15/ 2008
74. Too Many Secrets, Too Many Lies, Sonya Sparks $15.00
75. Stick And Move, Shawn Black ($15.00) Coming 1/15/ 2008
76. Evil Side Of Money, Jeff Robertson $15.00
77. Cater To Her, W.S Burkett $15.00 Coming 3/30/ 2008
78. Blood of my Brother, Zoe & Ysuf Woods $15.00
79. Hoodfellas, Richard Jeanty $15.00 11/30/2008
80. The Bedroom Bandit, Richard Jeanty $15.00 March 2009
81. Stick N Move II, Shawn Black $15.00 April 2009
82. Miami Noire, W.S. Burkett $15.00 June 2009
83. Insanely In Love, Cereka Cook $15.00 May 2009
84. Blood of My Brother III, Zoe & Yusuf Woods August 2009

Name_______________________________________
Address_____________________________________
City_______________State_____Zip Code_______

Please send the novels that I have circled above.

Shipping and Handling: Free
Total Number of Books__________
Total Amount Due______________

Buy 3 books and get 1 free. This offer is subject to change without notice.

Send institution check or money order (no cash or CODs) to:
RJ Publications
PO Box 300771
Jamaica, NY 11434

For more information please call 718-471-2926, or visit www.rjpublications.com

Please allow 2-3 weeks for delivery.

PUBLICATIONS
BRINGING EXCITEMENT, FUN AND JOY TO READING

PUBLICATIONS
BRINGING EXCITEMENT, FUN AND JOY TO READING